Chief Engineer B'Elanna Torres looked out on the same vast open area she had stood on seconds before. But now the area was filled with people, tall, thin humanoids of a kind she'd never seen before.

B'Elanna took in the scene for a moment and then tapped her comm badge. "Torres to *Voyager*. Come in, *Voyager*." There was no reply.

Fearing the worst, she took out her tricorder and checked the sky. *Voyager* was gone.

# Look for STAR TREK Fiction from Pocket Books

## Star Trek: The Original Series

# STAR TREK VOYAGER™

# The Escape

## Dean Wesley Smith and Kristine Kathryn Rusch

POCKET BOOKS

New York   London   Toronto   Sydney   Tokyo   Singapore

An *Original* Publication of POCKET BOOKS

POCKET BOOKS, a division of Simon & Schuster, Inc.
1230 Avenue of the Americas, New York, NY 10020

ISBN: 0-671-52096-2

First Pocket Books printing May 1995

10  9  8  7  6  5  4  3  2  1

POCKET and colophon are registered trademarks of
Simon & Schuster, Inc.

Printed in the U.S.A.

## Star Trek: The Next Generation

## Star Trek: Deep Space Nine

## Star Trek: Voyager

*For John Ordover,*
*a good friend and a wonderful editor*

# The Escape

# CHAPTER
# 1

THE SHUTTLE DIPPED AND BUCKED. CHIEF ENGINEER B'Elanna Torres kept her balance with practiced ease. She braced herself on the control panels with the heels of both hands. Her fingers dancing on the control panels like those of a concert pianist, constantly adjusting, strengthening, shifting power. She hadn't flown a Starfleet shuttle much since her Academy days, but it was coming back to her.

The mission should have been a simple one. The largest asteroid in this sector had deposits of armalcolite ore they needed to fix the Oltion circuits in the warp processor. Torres had convinced Captain Janeway to allow her to take a shuttlecraft to the asteroid for the necessary supplies. Sensors had shown an easy ride. In reality, the asteroid belt was as volatile as the Badlands had been. If Torres had known that before she started, she would have asked for Lieutenant Paris, the best pilot on *Voyager,* to join her.

Instead, the Vulcan security officer Tuvok sat in the pilot's seat. His brow was furrowed, making his eyebrows seem almost straight. He looked calm, but the beads of sweat on his forehead showed his tension. He wasn't the best pilot on board *Voyager,* but he was good.

They were so close. The sensors on *Voyager* had shown a high concentration of ore in the area, and Torres needed it. Desperately.

"I do not believe the shuttle can stand more of this." Tuvok spoke with his usual precision.

"I don't know if I can stand more of this." Torres shifted her hand onto the console and almost lost her balance. She wanted something to work right. Anything. She was tired of not having the right equipment or enough time to complete a task. It felt as if the entire Delta Quadrant were out to get her.

"Report." Captain Janeway's voice came clearly through the communications system of the bucking shuttlecraft. Torres almost snapped to attention, a habit she had thought lost until she met Janeway.

Torres glanced at the viewscreen. The asteroids surrounded their small ship like Cardassians around a helpless Bajoran. What had been a vision of hope a few hours ago was now a symbol of frustration.

"The subspace forces that tore this planet into an asteroid belt are still at work," she said, trying not to let that frustration into her voice. She wasn't as successful at it as Tuvok. But then she sometimes felt like she was all emotion while Tuvok was all intellect. "I'm not sure how much longer this craft can stand the punishment and I've found no way to block the disturbance."

"Thirty seconds to target," Tuvok said.

"I would suggest then, B'Elanna, that you and Mr. Tuvok return to the ship. We will determine how to get the ore from here."

"Captain, this will probably be our only chance."

Tuvok glanced at her, eyebrows raised in warning. She still wasn't used to the strictness of the command structure on a Starfleet vessel. "Twenty seconds," he said.

"It's your call, B'Elanna. But I don't want to lose two officers on a mission this minor."

B'Elanna opened her mouth to retort when Tuvok grabbed her arm. He shook his head.

No one seemed to understand how important this mission was to her. They needed the ore desperately for repairs to *Voyager*. She needed the ore. She was the one who worked two and three shifts straight jury-rigging all the equipment. If the captain had had to do all that work, she would never have called this mission minor.

The shuttle continued to rock in the subspace turbulence. Tuvok's steady hand kept them away from the larger asteroids, but the tiny ones pelted the shields.

"Captain, just a few more seconds—"

The interior lights of the shuttle dimmed for a

moment and B'Elanna's fingers flew over the control board. On the viewscreen, a large asteroid loomed in front of them.

"Report," the captain said.

The subspace turbulence was damaging the shuttle in ways B'Elanna didn't have time to fix. They were losing power and life support.

"The shuttle is not responding easily to my commands," Tuvok said.

B'Elanna cursed under her breath. If they didn't turn back now, they might never get the chance. The ore was important, but it wasn't worth losing the shuttle.

Or their lives.

"Let's get out of here," she said.

Tuvok nodded once as if any more movement would cause him to lose his precious control. He was hunched forward as if he could move the shuttle with the force of his will. Within seconds, he had the craft turned.

But it bounced and rolled. The turbulence seemed almost worse now that they were heading out of the field. Above Torres, something in the communications system released a slow, steady, irritating whine.

The lights dimmed again, then went out. The darkness in the craft made her clench her hand into a fist. Her left hand. She was still playing the controls with her right.

"Auxiliary power on," she said. The cabin lights flickered and came back on much dimmer than before. "Shields at only twenty percent. Don't hit anything too big."

"With the shields at twenty percent, even a small impact could prove disastrous." Tuvok spoke the obvious with the sincerity of a man giving a speech before the Federation. Next time, she would ask for Paris. He at least would not have the need to comment on every statement she made.

She leaned forward herself. The subspace turbulence had somehow grown worse. It was as if they were fighting back against a very real current where before they had been going with it. The shuttle rattled like a child's toy. It was coming apart.

"Captain," Torres said. "Life support is failing. The shuttle is disintegrating. Request you put a tractor beam on us."

"Done," Janeway said.

Now even Tuvok was sweating.

His fingers flew over the controls as fast as B'Elanna's.

Again the ship was buffeted by a wave of subspace disturbance, and then a loud crash echoed through the shuttle.

"What—?"

The lights went out again, then came back on. Sparks flew over both officers and the air filled with a thick smoke that smelled of burning insulation.

"That rock was 3.5 inches in diameter," Tuvok said in a matter-of-fact way.

"Shields at five percent." B'Elanna willed the shuttle forward. Instead of a fight to get into the belt, they were now in a race to get out. "I'm doing all I can, but I can't divert any more power. There simply isn't any."

Again the ship rocked and a smash echoed through the cabin. B'Elanna winced at the red light blinking on her console. "Hull breach in the rear cabin. We're sealed in."

The pressure door behind them slammed shut.

"That one was .53 inches," Tuvok said.

B'Elanna took a deep breath. Tuvok's calm seemed at times to almost be infectious. She let the level of her voice fall. "I'm holding five percent screens, but all life support is gone."

"B'Elanna. Mr. Tuvok." The captain's voice filled the smoky cabin. "As soon as we have a tractor on the shuttle, we'll beam you out."

The rattling of the hull and what seemed like every part inside it had become deafening. Tuvok's expert piloting kept them from the larger asteroids, and five percent screens at least blocked the smaller dust bits. But again something collided with the ship and sent it rocking.

"Twenty seconds," the captain said.

"I hope we have twenty seconds," B'Elanna said to herself. She wiped sweat from her eyes with the sleeve of her tunic. "I'm shutting down the engines and rerouting all power to the forward screens."

"Logical," Tuvok said. "But wait for my mark. I will aim for the clearest possible path."

He made a slight evasive action and something else crashed near the rear. "Now!"

Her fingers flew over the controls as she put all power to the shields. Beside her Tuvok's hands stopped and hovered over his dead panel.

"Sixty percent on the forward screens."

"Not enough." He pointed at the viewscreen ahead and the shuttle-sized rock hurtling at them.

*"Voyager!"* B'Elanna shouted. "Lock on that asteroid directly in our path and blow it out of space. Quick!"

"We see it." The captain sounded as calm as Tuvok. Didn't they feel the stress?

Every ounce of power B'Elanna could find in the poor, beat-up shuttle she directed at the forward shields, but she knew it would never be enough. That piece of rock was far, far too large.

Then, at what seemed to be the very last instant, she felt the tingle of a transporter. As she vanished she glanced at the viewscreen. It showed a phaser beam hitting the rough surface of the asteroid square in the center.

Captain Kathryn Janeway stood in the center of the bridge, feet apart, hands clasped behind her back. She was watching the asteroid explode on the viewscreen. The tractor beam around the tiny shuttle barely pulled it clear.

"Both officers on board, Captain." Ensign Hoffman's mellifluous voice sounded tinny through her comm link from the transporter room.

Janeway let out the breath she'd been holding. That had been just a little too close. So far from home, each routine action became a risk. She had hesitated before sending her experienced officers on a mission like this one, but now she was glad she had. She would definitely have lost two of the more inexperienced crew.

"Direct hit on the asteroid," said Ensign Harry Kim. For all his inexperience, Kim was already a good officer. "The shuttle is out of danger."

"Nice job, Ensign," Janeway said. Then she turned slightly to Lieutenant Tom Paris. "And nice job getting us in close. A fine piece of flying. Your quick action and skill may have saved their lives."

Paris let a smile cross his face without taking his eyes off his board. "Thank you, Captain."

Janeway held her position for a moment, the rigidity of her stance helping her control the fluttery feeling she had each time she remembered that the Federation *Starship Voyager* was all alone in the Delta Quadrant. She had flown missions without backup in the past, but she had always known that within a few days at warp speed, she could be at a Federation station or near a friendly planet. Not only was *Voyager* alone here, it was alone in uncharted space.

She knew that fact bothered the others, too, although they never spoke of it to her. Her first officer, Chakotay, simply wasn't the type. He stood behind Paris, as if he didn't trust Paris's expert flying. The two had an odd relationship, constantly bickering, and yet beneath it lay respect for each other's abilities. She had been lucky in both of them. She needed rebels and risk-takers out here. The average Starfleet officer would have had to learn some of the skills that came to these men as naturally as breathing.

She had been fortunate too in young Kim. He was so inexperienced in spaceflight that he adopted the attitude of the people around him. He was sharp and decisive, traits she valued more than she cared to name.

The bridge crew had returned to its morning business. Two other ensigns bent over the science station, deciphering information that came from the asteroid belt. A lieutenant stood in Tuvok's place near security, awaiting his return.

The expedition to the asteroid belt had provided the morning's excitement and nothing more.

Or so it seemed.

The expedition had pointed out several problems that Janeway had to deal with immediately.

"I want all senior officers in the briefing room at 0930," Janeway said as she headed for her ready room to prepare. "Commander Chakotay, you have the bridge until then."

The briefing room, like the rest of the ship, was done in gunmetal gray. Like everything else on *Voyager,* the room was designed for speed as well as comfort. Janeway felt each time she walked into the room that decisions made here would be swift, incisive, and important.

The soft conversation stopped as soon as she entered. Neelix and Kes sat on the far side of the table. Janeway's gaze was always drawn to their bright nonregulation clothing. They had shown their worth as guides and companions, and she did not regret bringing them on board.

Chakotay sat in his regular spot to the left of the captain's chair. He was a solid man, sturdy, like

*Voyager* herself. Paris sat on the other side of the table from Chakotay. Paris was not solid or sturdy, but mercurial and occasionally brilliant, hiding depths behind a soft, sardonic manner.

Finally her gaze rested on the two shuttle passengers. Tuvok sat calm and seemingly undisturbed by the morning's events. She was relieved to see him. She relied on his guidance more than she cared to admit.

She also relied on B'Elanna Torres. The chief engineer was smiling, a reaction that Janeway would not have expected. It seemed as if the near brush with death had lightened B'Elanna's outlook on life a little this morning.

Janeway took her place beside Chakotay.

"It seems," she said without preamble, "that we're not going to recover any ore from this asteroid belt. I will expect a full report on what happened as well as on the status of the shuttlecraft as soon as possible."

"You will have it within the hour," Tuvok said.

"Captain," B'Elanna said, "I already have Lieutenant Carey going over the shuttlecraft and starting what repairs he can."

"Good," Janeway said. She took a deep breath, then leaned forward slightly. "This morning's battle with the asteroid belt exemplifies the seriousness of our problems. We are short of most parts, the replicators are functioning only on an emergency basis, and the warp drive is down over fifty percent. Is that a fairly accurate assessment?"

She looked directly at B'Elanna, who for some reason looked relieved. B'Elanna must have thought that Janeway would do nothing about the engineering problems.

"Actually," B'Elanna said, "I don't think I can honestly guarantee more than another day of warp power until we find or manufacture some replacement parts. And that's if we take it easy on the drives. If we push them I wouldn't count on more than ten minutes."

Janeway nodded. "I agree, I'm afraid. I just—"

"You need parts for the engines of this ship?" Neelix asked. Apparently he hadn't understood what they had been talking about before. "Captain, you should have said so. Didn't I promise to take care of you?"

"Yes, Neelix," Janeway said, trying to keep the amusement out of her voice. "But you said that you weren't certain what type of ore we needed—"

"Ore." He made a chopping motion with his small, mottled hand. "I'm not talking about ore. You need parts for your ship and I know a place nearby where you can get plenty."

As if on cue every head in the room turned toward the short alien. He smiled and seemed to grow some under the attention. Kes proudly patted him on the leg.

"Do go on," Janeway said.

Neelix laughed and squeezed Kes's hand. "I'll take you to Alcawell. If you allow me to give you the coordinates, Captain—"

"Alcawell?" Paris asked. With that one word he managed to imply all sorts of questions. He also made it clear that the captain would not take coordinates until those questions were answered.

Janeway leaned back. The interaction among the crew had become predictable, and helpful.

Neelix never minded having the floor. "Alcawell translates roughly into *the Station.* But it's not a station. It's a planet. Many races in this area believe it to be sacred, a sort of home of the gods." He put an arm around Kes, almost as if his performance were for her and her alone. "But I've been there. It's no home for anyone."

"What's there that would help us?" Janeway asked.

"A lot of old ships. A *looootttt* of ships." Neelix smiled. "More ships than you have ever seen in your entire life."

"I doubt that," Paris said softly.

Neelix turned toward him, as if he needed to convince everyone. "Alcawell's been abandoned longer than any race in this area has been traveling space. They have so many ships that I'm sure one will help us. We can go in and take the parts we need out of the old wrecks. Or, perhaps, get the metals we need to make our own parts."

Interesting, but dangerous. Janeway leaned her head back on the chair. "You're telling us that you know of an old spaceport with a few abandoned ships? And no one has touched these ships?"

Neelix shrugged. "Who can tell if anyone has been near them? There are more ships than you can count. Believe me, a few parts won't be missed."

"We do not steal," Chakotay said. The firmness in his voice made Neelix shrink a little.

He frowned as if considering, then grinned. "Once you see the place I doubt you would call it stealing. More like salvaging."

"Under your definition of salvage?" Paris asked. "Or ours?"

This time Neelix ignored him. Neelix fixed his catlike gaze on Janeway. She, at least, wanted to see the station.

"To what race did this base belong?" Tuvok asked.

"I don't know," Neelix said, "but they've been gone for centuries."

Tuvok templed his fingers and tapped them against his lips. "If it's such a good place to salvage," he asked slowly, "why haven't you gone back there?"

Neelix pulled Kes closer. She watched him in her calm, intent way. When it looked like he wasn't going to answer, she nodded at him to continue.

He tilted his head, raised his bushy eyebrows, and shrugged again. "Honestly, I—" He sighed and dipped his head so that they couldn't see his expression. "I think the station's haunted."

Paris snorted and sat back in his chair as if he had expected something like that all along. Tuvok didn't move, but Janeway could sense his sudden dismissal of the plan.

Only B'Elanna still looked interested. "But there are a lot of old ships."

Neelix brought his head up. "Yes."

"Abandoned ships."

"Yes."

"Captain," B'Elanna said. "If we—"

But Neelix interrupted her. "Captain, if there aren't

more ships abandoned on Alcawell than you would care to count, you can leave me behind with the ghosts."

"And me too," Kes said softly.

"Thank you, my love," Neelix said, squeezing her hand. He turned to the others. "Isn't she remarkable?"

Janeway made a decision. They couldn't afford to overlook any opportunity. "I think we should see Alcawell for ourselves. What say you, Mr. Tuvok?"

"I would agree, Captain."

Janeway glanced at her first officer. Chakotay nodded in agreement.

Satisfied, Janeway stood. "Neelix, give Lieutenant Paris the coordinates for Alcawell. B'Elanna, I would like to get there quickly but without further damaging the warp engines. What do you recommend?"

"Warp one," B'Elanna said.

Janeway turned to Paris and nodded. "Get us under way, mister."

Paris slid his chair back and motioned for Neelix to follow him onto the bridge.

As they left Janeway faced her remaining officers. "Salvage or not, we need the parts. At this point we're in no position to be proud."

Then she smiled as she stood. "Besides, who's afraid of a few ghosts?"

# CHAPTER
# 2

CAPTAIN JANEWAY SAT AT HER DESK IN THE READY ROOM, going over reports on a padd. At times, she wished that she could jettison the busy work associated with the captaincy. But for each bit of routine that she dispensed with, a bit of home went with it. She had already made decisions that would never have been made in the Alpha Quadrant.

Occasionally she glanced at the long windows showing a view of the stars. Sometimes she wished the positions were familiar. Sometimes she was pleased they were not.

"Captain." Ensign Kim's voice broke her concentration. "We are over the Station."

"Excellent, Ensign," she said. "I'll—"

But he didn't wait for her to finish. "And I think you need to take a look at this."

She smiled at the tone of fascination and awe in Harry Kim's voice. Perhaps there was something to Neelix's wild claims. She hoped so. *Voyager* had limped to Alcawell and Janeway had worried that she was using the last of their power for a wild chase after nothing.

She placed the padd on her desk and stood, brushing her hair with the heel of one hand, making certain not a strand was out of place. Then she left the ready room and stepped onto the bridge.

Paris sat immobile at conn, Chakotay was sitting on the edge of the captain's chair, and Tuvok stood at his station in tactical. All stared, transfixed, at the main viewscreen. Her gaze followed theirs, and her mouth opened involuntarily. She shut it quickly, glad no one had seen her. But the feeling that had caused the reaction remained.

Row after row, kilometer after kilometer of ships filled the viewscreen. They went off the edge of the screen in all directions.

She made herself limit down her focus. Each ship seemed to be identical to the others, round with three slender tripod legs as a sort of landing gear. The ships were spaced an even distance from each other.

She pulled her focus back to the entire screen again. The rows of ships seemed to go on forever in all directions. How was this possible? She was having real trouble grasping the scale of what she was seeing. They looked almost like children's toys lined up neatly. Yet they were all real. Very real.

"Captain." Kim was standing in operations, his fingers poised over the screen controls. "From what I can tell, this is the largest of four—ah, I suppose you could call them bases. Or maybe ports? There seems to be a base or port in the middle of each of the continents on this planet."

"Are there life signs?" Chakotay asked.

Kim looked away from the screen, tapped the ops panel before him, and read the results. Then he shook his head. "Nothing above rodent size."

"Captain," Tuvok said. "There are extensive remains of a humanoid civilization scattered over the planet, but nothing as preserved as these ships appear to be. There are also large building ruins scattered between the ships at regular intervals. No ship is very far from what was once a building. A very efficient design and use of space."

"What's the size of this?" Janeway asked, not taking her gaze from the screen. "I have no sense of scale."

Tuvok nodded. "This facility alone is twice the size of the Federation's Luna Station. One-eighth of Vulcan would be covered in these ships if all four bases, as Mr. Kim called them, were combined."

"This base, or station, is square," Janeway said, trying to put this in a perspective she understood. "You're telling me, Tuvok, that if we put the northwestern corner of this base in Federation Headquarters in San Francisco, the edges of the base would stretch south to the center of Los Angeles and east to Reno?"

Paris whistled.

"Yes, Captain," Tuvok said, "although I doubt the ships would line up as neatly on Earth." He took a deep breath. Janeway recognized the pause. He made one just like it each time he imparted information that had an element of speculation to it. "And one more thing. These ships were never meant to fly, at least not by any means we know of."

"What?" Janeway spun to look at Tuvok. His steady gaze met hers. He understood her sudden excitement. Neelix had led them to a technology they hadn't seen before. Janeway slapped her comm badge. "B'Elanna, are you studying the ships onscreen?"

B'Elanna had spent the trip in Engineering, coaxing all the power she could out of the warp engines. "Yes, Captain."

"Do you have any idea what they were?"

"Not from here, Captain. Without a hands-on inspection I couldn't even tell you what their power source was, let alone what their function might have been. But I can confirm that the metals in the ships' bodies and engines are ones we need for repairs."

"Captain." Kim had moved to the science station. "The ruins around the ports are layered as far back as I can get readings. And this is a very, very old planet."

"So," Janeway said, turning back to stare at the incredible sight of square kilometers of ships parked side by side, "we're talking about the home of a very old race that moved on, or maybe died out a long time ago?"

"It would seem that way," Chakotay said.

"Things are not always as they seem," Tuvok said.

"Go on."

"There is no logic in this situation," Tuvok said. "The ships are obviously quite old, yet they are in a better state of repair than any of the surrounding ruins, including the buildings spaced evenly throughout the port."

"Your conclusion?" Janeway asked.

"I have no conclusion," Tuvok said. "But it is possible that the owners of the ships and the inhabitants of the ruins may not be one and the same."

Janeway nodded. She paused a moment, then made a decision. She again tapped her comm badge. "B'Elanna, I would like you to study one of the ships firsthand."

"Aye, aye, Captain." B'Elanna sounded eager. Janeway smiled. She envied the Engineer her mobility. Janeway herself would have loved to be the first to visit Alcawell.

She turned to Ensign Kim. "Find Neelix. I want the two of you to join her." Beside her Chakotay nodded at her choice of away team in agreement. Kim would keep Torres level. Neelix would go along for local information in case they found anything on the old ships he might recognize.

Kim headed across the bridge for the door. He too clearly felt the same excitement. If this station was as promising as it looked, they might discover some new technology to help them find a way home. Or clearly at least give them the raw materials to make repairs.

"And Mr. Kim."

He stopped and turned to face her. "Yes, Captain?"

"Your job is to guard her back while she works and keep Neelix out of trouble. Understand?"

He smiled slightly. "Understood, Captain."

Janeway said to Tuvok, "You have five minutes to search that haystack down there for a working ship. I want you to be ready to send them to that ship when they gather in the transporter room."

Then she turned back to stare at the viewscreen. Ships, parked in neat rows, extended beyond visible range. Thousands and thousands of ships. "They're never going to believe this when we get home," she said.

# CHAPTER
# 3

THE TRANSPORTER DROPPED THEM ON A HARD, CONCRETE-like surface near the south edge of the Station. Cold wind cut at B'Elanna's uniform and bits of sand nipped her face. The air smelled stale, and her mouth dried almost instantly from the total lack of humidity. The entire place had a feeling of age and death that chilled her far more than did the biting wind.

She glanced quickly around, then just stopped and stared at the parked ships in complete amazement. One after another, side by side, the ships stretched into the distance like images in facing mirrors. At first glance they all seemed to be exactly the same, and she could tell from the dozens that towered around them that they were very, very old. Some had weathered the years better than others in the constant wind and sand.

To her left one had tipped slightly where its short, stemlike landing gear had given way. When fully upright, the ships were held about four meters above the ground on tripod legs. A fairly gentle-sloped ramp extended down from the center of each ship like a giant tongue. They'd have no problems getting inside the ships, because they were all standing open.

She looked slowly around, studying the wrecks. One ship had a small hole in its side that looked as if something inside had exploded and ruptured the gray hull. But all in all the ships had lasted much, much better than the ruins of a building a hundred meters away. She couldn't tell for sure, but she thought she could see faint markings on the concrete surface scoured by the years of sand. The markings seemed to lead from the bottom of each ship's ramp toward the building.

The view from *Voyager* had given her a sense of scale for the station itself, but not for the ships. Each ship was about two times larger than a Federation shuttlecraft. They were like slightly flattened round balls. Even on their short legs they towered over her. The landing legs alone were twice her width, yet under the weight of the ships they looked thin.

She did a slow, full circle turn just taking in the ships that hung precariously above and around her and stretched off into the distance in all directions. Large alien machinery, toppling under the pressure of time and wind, in a very alien setting.

Drifts of sand had formed around the bases of a few of the nearby ships and the ramps leading up into them. The wind made a strange whistling sound that sent shivers down B'Elanna's back.

She flipped open her tricorder. Ensign Kim did the same. The best way to fight the oddness of this place was to focus on work, and that was exactly what she would do.

"Ghosts. Spirits. The undead. The past walks here," Neelix said, almost shouting to be heard over the wind. "Can't you feel it?" He wrapped his arms tight around himself. "I don't know why I'm even here. And it's cold. Very cold. Maybe I should beam up and get us all coats."

"You're staying with us," B'Elanna said, her voice crisp. She didn't need any distractions.

Neelix huffed, but said nothing.

Her scan showed no life signs and no obvious traps. Nothing but an abandoned field of old ships that were never intended to fly through air or space. Strange. Everything about this place was strange.

She turned to her right and did a more careful scan of the ship Tuvok had picked out for them. It seemed to be a good choice. The hull was the same dull weathered gray as the rest, but she could see no obvious damage. Her readings indicated that this ship was no different from the rest, but somehow it felt newer than the others.

"Let's see what the inside looks like," she said.

"Good," Kim said. "This blowing sand really hurts."

She glanced over at him and Neelix. Both had turned their backs to the wind and were protecting their eyes. Getting out of the wind would be a good idea.

Holding her tricorder in front of her and scanning for any signs of traps or life-forms, she moved to the ramp under the center of the ship and looked up. The incline was gentle and the ramp was grooved to keep users from slipping. The door at the top was wide open and B'Elanna could see a wall beyond with a faded red arrow pointing to the right. A small drift of sand had formed around the base of the ramp.

"This had a lot of traffic once," Kim said, scanning his tricorder over the ramp.

"Traffic?" Neelix asked, looking around as if he could see the traffic nearby.

"Passengers would be my guess," Kim said. "The design and the wear patterns indicate this boarding ramp was well used."

"Used for what is the question," B'Elanna said.

Kim shrugged. "This place reminds me of a shuttleport back home. Sort of." He kept staring at his tricorder.

"It reminds me how much I hate being cold," Neelix said. "And how my quarters are warm and dry."

B'Elanna walked up the wide ramp to the opening, holding her tricorder in front of her. She wanted to draw her phaser, but knew that would seem stupid under the circumstances. Nothing had threatened them. There didn't seem to be anything on this planet that could threaten them. But she still would rather have a phaser in her hand than a tricorder the way her stomach was twisting. She would just feel better.

"The ship's empty," Kim said.

"Of course it's empty," Neelix said. "These are all abandoned ships." He stepped around Kim and B'Elanna, and before either of them could stop him he walked calmly inside and down the wide corridor indicated by the faded arrow.

Indirect lighting flickered on marking the way as he walked.

"Neelix!" B'Elanna shouted.

"It's warm in here!" he said.

"Amazing," Kim said, studying his tricorder. "Lights and power source still functioning after all this time."

"Yeah," B'Elanna said, scanning her tricorder for any signs of danger before following Neelix.

The passageway was about ten meters long and turned sharply to the left into a large room with bench seats around the outside and other seats attached to chairs in groupings throughout the room. The room was larger than some Maquis ships. Over a hundred passengers could fit comfortably in this space.

Neelix stood in the middle with his hands open. "See? Empty, just as I told you."

"There are no other rooms," Kim said. "How did they pilot this thing?"

"All empty tin cans," Neelix said. "Good for salvage, huh?"

"There isn't even an engine room," Kim said. "Or for that matter, an engine."

"Just don't touch anything," B'Elanna said, staring directly at Neelix. "At least until we determine what these ships were and what controls them."

Neelix sighed and sat down on the nearest chair, leaning back and putting his feet up. "At least we're out of the wind in here."

"Look at this," Kim said, pointing at a blinking red sign over the passageway they had just come in. The sign was in an unidentifiable language with a numberlike sequence that kept changing. "It started blinking when Neelix sat down."

"See if you can figure out what it says," B'Elanna said. She tapped her comm badge. "Away team to *Voyager.*"

"*Voyager* here," Janeway's voice answered.

"We're inside. No signs of life. The ship still has an automatic power source of some sort that we somehow triggered on entering."

"Can you tell what the ships were used for?" Janeway asked.

"Passenger transport of some type. The insides are nothing more than a large room with benches and chairs. But I can't imagine where these could go. Or for that matter, how. It will take me some time to figure this out."

"Passenger?" Janeway said, more to herself than B'Elanna. "Well, be careful and report as soon as you have something."

"Understood," B'Elanna said.

"Any luck, Mr. Kim?" B'Elanna asked.

"It looks like a time sequence to me, but I'm operating on guesswork."

"Neelix," B'Elanna said, turning to the short alien lounging with his eyes half closed. "Do you recognize that language?" She pointed to the flashing sign over the entry.

He opened one eye and studied the message, then sat up. "I have a vague memory of something similar to that. It's a very dead language, though. That much I can tell you."

"But can you read it?" B'Elanna asked. She didn't have time for games.

He shrugged. "I think it says *Please Take a Seat.*"

"And the numbers?" Kim said.

"Just numbers," Neelix said. He leaned back and closed his eyes. "Let me know when you need my help again. I will be napping."

B'Elanna shook her head at Neelix and turned to Kim. "Link with *Voyager*'s computer, feed that information into it, and see what comes up. I'm going to look for the—"

The number sequence on the sign over Kim's head stopped and the room's lights flashed once. A scraping noise echoed through the ship and it shuddered slightly.

"The ramp is coming up!" Kim shouted and started for the door.

"Wait!" B'Elanna's command stopped him in his tracks. "Stay together." She slapped her comm badge. *"Voyager.* The ship is coming to life and closing up. Be ready to beam us out of here on my mark."

"Understood," Tuvok's calm voice answered back. "We have a transporter lock on you."

"Mr. Kim," B'Elanna said. "See if you can find what's causing this. We'll stay as long as we can. Neelix, help him." She scanned with her tricorder, but couldn't find the ship's power source. There had to be one. Somewhere.

A huge clang echoed through the ship. The clang was followed by painful screech as of metal scraping against metal without lubrication.

"The door is closed and the ship's lifting off the surface," Kim said, panic in his voice.

Then the air shimmered slightly and the ship settled back to the surface with a slight thud.

"The door is opening," Kim said. Over his head the sign again started to flash.

"Fast trip that one," Neelix said. He sounded calm, but he was standing now and had somehow moved right next to B'Elanna.

B'Elanna studied her tricorder, but all the readings indicated that nothing had changed with the ship. It had simply closed the door, lifted less than a meter off the ground, then settled back into place. But why? Had the trip been aborted? And how had it even lifted? There were no signs of antigravity units on this ship, or even engines. Nothing but a huge waiting room.

Suddenly B'Elanna realized something was very different. A draft of almost hot air blew in the corridor and the light from the direction of the door looked brighter.

Kim had already noticed and had his tricorder

pointed at the entrance to the ship. "There's something wrong here," he said softly.

B'Elanna turned her tricorder in the same direction and got the answer. The air coming in the open door was totally different from when they had come in. It had more organisms in it. And humidity. And it was warmer. Considerably warmer.

With Kim and Neelix at her side, she moved cautiously toward the entrance. When they reached the point at the top of the ramp where they could see out, they stopped.

And stared.

"Oh, my," Neelix said.

"Where are we?" Kim asked.

Spread out in front of them was the same vast open area, only now most of the ships were gone. The pavement was covered with fresh colored lines. The buildings looked new. Tall, thin humanoids walked at different speeds to and from the ships and the building.

The people dressed in bright greens, reds, and purples. Most wore blue or yellow hats that somehow failed to clash. Some humanoids walked alone. Others walked in groups. Some carried what appeared to be luggage, while others carried nothing.

Ten ships down, a door silently closed and a ramp pulled up. The ship lifted off the pavement and vanished.

None of the nearby humanoids seemed to notice at all.

B'Elanna took in the scene for a moment and then

tapped her comm badge. "Away team to *Voyager*. Come in, *Voyager*."

No answer.

Kim quickly adjusted his tricorder and then in a cracking voice told her what she already feared.

"*Voyager* is no longer in orbit."

# CHAPTER
## 4

JANEWAY DID NOT LIKE THE FACT THAT THREE OF HER CREW
members were inside a ship whose power had just
come on. She stood in the center of the bridge,
Chakotay beside her, Paris at conn, and stared at the
viewscreen as if it provided answers. It did not. The
view was the same: row after row of ships extended far
into the distance. If she had not known that her people
were aboard the ship directly in the center of the
screen, she would not have been able to discern their
presence at all.

Tuvok was monitoring their progress. "The ship is
lifting," he said.

Janeway hit her comm badge. Ensign Hoffman was
the best transporter operator they had. If anyone
could get them out quickly, Ensign Hoffman could.

"Transporter room," Janeway said. "Get them out of there."

"Aye, sir." Ensign Hoffman always resorted to Starfleet protocol when rattled.

Janeway was rattled herself. She didn't want any of her crew to get hurt. Who would have thought that ancient ships would have started so easily? Or so mysteriously?

"The ship has disappeared," Paris said. His normally sardonic voice had an element of surprise in it.

"Confirmed, Captain." Even Tuvok sounded a bit odd. He clearly hadn't expected this either.

Janeway could see that the ship had disappeared. What had been an unbroken row of tiny circular ships a moment before was now a row of tiny circular ships with one ship-sized break in the middle.

"Transporter room?" Janeway said. "Ensign Hoffman, did you get them?"

Silence greeted her. Janeway hit her comm badge again.

"Ensign Hoffman! Report!"

Chakotay looked at Janeway. His broad features were stern. There was no comfort in his expression.

"I'm sorry, Captain." Hoffman's soft voice had a note of regret. "The link was broken. I can't seem to get a fix on them."

Janeway turned to Tuvok. "Can you trace them? Where'd the ship go?"

Tuvok's hands were already playing the board. Chakotay sprinted to the science station, and Paris was manipulating information on conn.

"I can't trace them," Chakotay said.

"It's not possible," said Paris.

"It happened," Tuvok said. "Therefore it is possible."

"Save the debate for another time, gentlemen," Janeway said. "Tell me what has happened to my away team."

Chakotay shook his head. "I'm afraid I can't, Captain."

"Captain," Paris said. "That ship and the three aboard no longer exist in this place and time."

"They no longer *exist?*" Janeway asked. "Are they dead?"

"I don't know, Captain," Tuvok said, "although that is doubtful. The ship vanished. They vanished with it."

"I know that," Janeway said. "I want to know what happened to it."

"Believe me, Captain, we do too," Paris said. He was staring at the board in front of him as if it could provide answers.

"It was not destroyed or transported by any means we know," Chakotay said. "It is not cloaked and it did not leave the planet in any normal fashion."

"So what happened to it?" Janeway asked.

Tuvok looked up and held her gaze for a moment before he answered. "It just simply ceased to exist."

"Gentlemen, I do not accept that explanation. My away team has disappeared. We will find them." Janeway climbed the steps to the science station herself. As she stepped beside Chakotay, he made a startled sound.

"Captain," all three men said together. Paris finished the sentence. "The ship's back."

Janeway looked at the viewscreen. The tiny hole in the rows of ships was gone. She let out the breath she had been holding. She tapped her comm badge.

"Ensign Hoffman, beam that team out of there," she said.

"Wait, Captain," Chakotay said. "Better belay that order."

"Hold, Ensign." Janeway turned to Chakotay. "This had better be good."

"There's only one person on board," Chakotay said.

"Humanoid," Tuvok added.

"But no one we know," Paris said.

"No one we know?" Janeway asked. She moved in beside Chakotay. The evidence at the science station was incontrovertible. The ship had left seconds earlier with all three members of the away team. It had reappeared with a single person on board, but that person wasn't human or a member of any other race the Federation had ever met.

The away team had completely vanished. Not a trace of them was left.

The warmth of the day and the heat coming off the concrete surface below the ramp contrasted sharply with the memory Torres had of this same place just a few minutes before. Cold winds and sand had blown thin air through thousands of abandoned ships. The sky had been a dull gray above the ship graveyard and the sun not much more than a low glow on the horizon.

Now the day was warm, the light yellow, the sky clear, and the sun directly overhead. The ships all seemed to be new, at least those that were present.

And in a place where before no one had existed, not one living thing, now teemed thousands of colorfully dressed humanoids, calmly going about their business between the ships and the buildings. These humanoids all appeared to belong to the same race: they were as tall as most Klingons, but had larger chins and smaller foreheads. They seemed, however, to vary as much as Klingons varied. Like Earthlings, though, these people had different-color hair and a finer bone structure. Their clothing was as varied as their personal appearances. But nothing about them gave any clue as to what they used the ships for.

B'Elanna set the shock of change aside—getting lost in the reaction would do her no good—and took a hard look up at the underside of the ship they had arrived in. It was clearly the same one, old and very weathered. The ships around them seemed much newer. She turned to Kim. His eyes were wide, his skin unnaturally pale. He had looked this same way when she had first met him, in the Ocampa doctor's rooms. Superficially composed and yet clearly scared to death.

She knew he could function in strange circumstances. Despite his youth, he had strength. The secret was to tap it.

"Find out where we are," she said, her voice almost a whisper, as if she was afraid someone might hear them.

Kim glanced down at his tricorder. "How do I even start?" he asked, also very softly.

"Start with the ships beside us, then go to the people." B'Elanna really didn't really care what order he worked in, so she had given him the order that seemed the simplest. Although here nothing seemed simple. And they all would have to be thinking clearly, and acting quickly.

Behind her, Neelix hadn't moved at all. His tiny, spotted hands grasped the edge of the door. His knuckles were white. "You all right?" she asked.

"Ghosts," he said. "Look at all the ghosts. I told you this place was haunted."

"I doubt those are ghosts," B'Elanna said. "Mr. Kim?"

Kim nodded. "They are very real. Everything here is real." He sounded as if he had hoped he was dreaming. No such luck.

Two men and a woman, all wearing bright green smocks over purple pantaloons, stopped in front of a ship three down. They were talking and laughing. The woman had silver hair piled over a meter above her head. One of the men motioned at it. She nodded and took the hair off, revealing a head of black hair closely cut to her scalp. Then she tucked the silver wig under her arm and climbed the boarding ramp to the ship. The men followed her.

"Clearly the ship took us somewhere," B'Elanna said. "And it used a method faster than any we know. Kim, find out where, and how far away from *Voyager* we are."

Kim silently did as he was told, his handsome face a

picture of concentration. B'Elanna wiped a bead of sweat off her neck. Ten minutes ago she was wishing she had worn a coat; now she wished she had on her lighter uniform.

"The surrounding star positions are the same," Kim said. He sounded uncertain. "Sort of."

"'Sort of'?" Torres asked. "Can you be a little more specific than 'sort of'?"

He glanced up at her. She recognized the look. She had seen it on his face when they were walking through the Ocampa settlement underground, soon after they had been forced to come to the Delta Quadrant. He was still new enough to space travel to find most things unbelievable. A drawback some days. A benefit others. She waited, uncertain which it would be this time.

"I want to say I'm looking at the same stars as I was before we got onto the ship. We're still in the Delta Quadrant, but—"

"Mr. Kim," Torres said, "I don't need an astronomy lesson. I asked you to define 'sort of.' Define it. This is not an essay exam. This isn't even an exam. It's a simple question."

"But the answer's not that simple. The stars are exactly where they should be, if they were younger. It's as if—" He stopped, apparently unable to finish.

B'Elanna understood. She didn't want to, but she thought she understood. She quickly used her own tricorder to do the figuring as Kim did the same. Within a few seconds she had the answer.

"Three hundred and ten thousand years," she said softly.

"What?" Neelix said. He had taken his hands off the door and was wringing them together. "Three hundred and ten thousand years what?"

The edge of panic in his voice echoed the feeling in B'Elanna's stomach. She decided to ignore that feeling. It would get in her way. She made her voice as calm as Tuvok's. She was beginning to understand how the Vulcan and the captain managed to sound relaxed even under stress. "We've jumped into the past of this planet by three hundred and ten thousand years," she said.

"That's not possible," Neelix said. He moved away from her until his back hit the frame of the ship. Then he tugged on the flamboyant shirt he wore. "Frankly, if it's all the same to you, I would prefer to believe in ghosts. Yes. Let's make all these people ghosts. Ghosts are a much better idea than time travel, don't you agree?"

Torres wasn't sure if she did agree. Now that she was getting past her shock, she was finding this situation fascinating. She was slowly starting to understand just a part of what this huge facility was and she was growing very, very impressed.

These ships were time shuttles.

All these people around them were traveling through time as if it were commonplace. And from the looks of this station, it was. Somehow they had boarded a working shuttle in the far, dead future and got sent here, to this time.

"I'm afraid that we have to rule out the ghosts, Neelix, and accept time travel. It's our only chance to get back home," Torres said. She turned to Kim. "We had to have done something to trigger this ship to jump. We need to find that trigger."

"How about if I just go back inside and wait for you folks to come up with an answer. I missed a good nap to be here. I wouldn't mind sleeping my way through your solution. In fact, that sounds very good. I'm going back inside now." Neelix backed through the door, keeping his gaze on the strange people around him.

"Don't touch anything," B'Elanna said. "Just go back in and sit—" She stopped suddenly. A clear picture went through her mind of Neelix plopping down on the ship. "Check the seat that Neelix sat in. There might be sensors in the chairs."

"Let's do it quickly," Neelix said, and nodded in the direction of the bottom of the ramp. One of the humanoids, a tall man wearing a bright orange jump suit, stood with his hands on his hips looking stern and slowly shaking his head at them.

At closer look B'Elanna could see that he had bright blue eyes, set very wide on his face, a nose that seemed almost smashed flat, and at least eight fingers. The orange coveralls did very little to mask his strength of upper body. B'Elanna thought the size of him would compare well to a Klingon warrior's.

"You are not authorized to be here," the man said.

Torres replaced her tricorder and held out her hands in what she hoped was a universal gesture of conciliation. "We know," she said. "We—"

"You have to come to Control."

"Actually," she said. "We'd rather go back. We didn't expect—"

"Your appearance here is a violation of Control Ordinance 852.61."

"We're sorry," Kim said. He glanced at B'Elanna. "We didn't mean to. We accidentally triggered—"

"Any eight-hundred violation requires the presence of the violators at Control. If you don't come with me voluntarily, we'll take you by force."

"We volunteer!" Neelix said, holding up his hands as he came out of the ship. "We volunteer, don't we, friends?"

Torres sighed. She never volunteered to get into trouble, yet it always seemed to happen.

"Let's move," the man said. "We need to deal with this violation quickly. That ship has to be off the platform in three hours. We're expecting the Real Time ship to return then."

Torres glanced at her companions, hoping they understood better than she did. Kim shrugged. Neelix had his hands above his head and was marching forward, following the strange man. When Neelix got off the ramp he stopped beside the man. He barely came to the man's waist.

Torres could see Neelix's strangeness register on the man's face; then it seemed to fade into unimportance.

"Hurry," the man said. He whirled and walked away as if he expected them to follow him.

"It seems we have no choice," Torres said. She indicated that Kim should be first behind the man in orange. Neelix dropped into line next and she brought up the rear, carefully marking in her mind exactly how to get back to the exact ship they had arrived in.

She just hoped she got the chance.

# CHAPTER
# 5

THE ALARM CHIMED THROUGH THE WARM INTERIOR OF Drickel's hilltop home, rousing him from his afternoon nap on his favorite couch. That alarm hadn't gone off in years and he'd almost forgotten how much its soft, gentle chimes annoyed him.

"All right, all right," he said. "Alarm off."

The chimes stopped and the faint lyrical sounds of Period Three flutes filled the house with soothing harmonies from the best musicians of Rollingburg's Retreat.

He yawned, rubbed his eyes, and sat up. The green of the living room, with its scattered sofas and seating arrangements, blended into the green of the plush jungle outside. The walls were large windows that provided him with a clear view of dozens of different animals. Beyond the jungle, he could see a range of tall, new, and very rough mountains in the distance. Some days he focused the window on the mountains. During others, he buried the view deep into the forest. Before he had gone to sleep, he left the view turned to a shadowy undergrowth that let in little light. The cool, moist darkness looked inviting, but he had an alarm to answer.

He cursed silently and dialed up a broader view. The day itself was warm and sunny and the mountains beckoned in the distance. Often he woke himself by exploring the top of the mountain range, focusing on water, and letting the sparkle take him. The diversity was one reason why he had settled in this Period. He loved the peacefulness of it. Chasing damn alarms made him angry.

After six-point-seven years of Real Time, he still got angry. That last alarm had taken almost two days of his Real Time and forced him to go to a cold Period during winter months. It took almost a week of Real Time after his return to shake the trauma of the experience from his bones.

He had received a commendation for that little adventure. But the commendation had been small recompense for the days of chill. Saunas, steam baths, and cutting wood in the hot jungle sun hadn't warmed him. He finally had to ask Medical for a balm to get the winter out of his system.

No use complaining. The alarm had sounded and he had to respond. He supposed he shouldn't be so angry at earning his salary now and then. Without the Watchman job he would never have afforded this beautiful house.

He stood, stretching his tall frame and loosening tight muscles. He had just finished his first workout of the day before his nap. His loose-fitting green warm-up suit was a bit gamy, and his headband had stuck to his forehead.

With one last longing glance at the lush jungles and the rocky mountains in the distance, he tapped a seven-digit code into a small console on the wall near the entrance to his kitchen. He used the console every day to report in. Food and supplies also came thanks to that console, and occasionally he received calls from friends. But it felt odd to his fingers to be punching in his security code again.

He first looked for a date on the readout, then sighed. Of course they would send him somewhere cold and dark. Seven and a half million years in the future. Couldn't someone mess with the Time Stations in the summer months? Probably not.

The stations were abandoned after the Second Expansion Period and the ships looked ripe for the taking. At least he wouldn't have to deal with his own kind. There were only a few really crazy folks who lived that far up the time line, and most of them were a million or so years even farther into the future. Real nut cases who seemed to find the desertlike periods enjoyable.

Much as he hated where he was heading, he appreciated the fact that he would be alone. His own people sometimes interfered when faced with an interloper. Better to handle it alone. Much better.

Maybe he would earn another commendation.

Another commendation would bring a significant

raise in pay. He would be able to install view windows in the west wing of the house.

Enough dreaming. He had to respond to the alarm first. The readout showed that no one had lived anywhere near the alarm for thousands of Real Time years.

He'd had some experience with this specific Period. The only creatures that triggered alarms were Planet-Hoppers. They were always the most difficult to handle. Their cultures were sophisticated enough to allow them to travel through space, but still primitive enough to limit that travel to physical movement.

Often Planet-Hoppers would see things like the old Time Stations as places to be plundered, thinking them truly abandoned. The last time he had been to this specific Period he had spent five Real Time days howling like a jungle cat before realizing that the Planet-Hoppers thought the wind made the sound.

Fortunately he had other tricks that sent those nosy little Planet-Hoppers back to their Vacuum Ships.

He tapped in his response code, informing the Mean Time Control that he was headed for the alarm, then turned and walked quickly through the comfortable green hallways to his bedroom. There, he double-checked the readout on the secondary display.

Of course. A part of the planet and a time of year there almost as cold as his previous alarm. He would need all of his warm clothing.

"Why couldn't these trespassers pick the summer side? Or at least springside?" he muttered. "Would that be too much to ask?"

Since he had lived alone for the past sixteen years of his Real Time, no one answered him.

He tossed his pack into his bedroom transport booth, and punched in passage to the closest Time Station. His only hope was that he could make this mission quick.

The inside of the building was even warmer than outside. Torres brushed hair off her ridged forehead and wondered how she had ever felt cold. Kim gasped beside her. Neelix, mercifully, was silent.

The orange-suited man who had brought them here herded them together as if they were Romulan sheep. He didn't have to. All three of them had stopped once they came through the door.

The building was unlike what Torres had expected, although if anyone had asked her what she had expected, she would have been unable to answer. She had not expected the teeming mass of people. So many people, in fact, that they had ceased being individuals and had become a sea of color and sound, moving back and forth like waves. Concentrating on the people was too overwhelming. She concentrated on the building instead.

The man had brought them into a huge hall with staircases on its north and south faces. The ceiling was twice as high as the ceilings in *Voyager,* and it was a sparkly white. After a moment, she realized that what she had taken as sparkles were actually tiny lights embedded into the ceiling tiles. The white motif went throughout the building with limited success. Once the white reached shoulder height of these odd people, dirt and smudges marred it. Tiny drawings covered the floor. At first Torres thought the drawings graffiti. Then she realized that they were diagrams leading the first-time traveler to the booths that clustered together in various segments of the huge hall.

"Transport booths," Kim said, his voice hushed slightly in awe. He was looking in the same direction as Torres was.

She nodded. The transporters were encased by clear walls, and serviced only one person at a time. But it was clear they operated on the same principle as the unit in *Voyager*. All the booths were painted in bright colors and had signs over them. One person entered on one side, while another would leave from a different side. They would hesitate only as they entered, pausing to punch in a quick code on a panel on the outside, before stepping inside and vanishing. Torres was very impressed, especially considering how many thousands and thousands of these building remains *Voyager* had seen during their scans from space.

Some of the booths had short lines waiting to get in. Others were empty. Torres guessed that each booth went to transporter booths in a certain area of the planet.

The people who used the booths had purposeful but blank expressions on their faces. Torres recognized the look. She had used it herself when taking the same route day after day. Almost everyone using the booths carried a small case. Some people were with families. Others alone. Torres had seen this exact scene hundreds of times throughout the Federation. This was a transportation facility. Some of the people were going to or from work, others were traveling on vacation or business.

Only outside the doors of this terminal weren't shuttles to take the travelers into orbit or to another part of the planet. Outside these doors was a huge field of ships that seemed to travel in time. That meant all these people were commuting through time in some fashion or another. She had no idea how the society worked, how it dealt with all the time paradoxes, or even why it would risk such difficulties.

She wanted to find out.

Neelix had apparently seen enough. He bounced on his feet, catching the attention of the man in orange. "Are you taking us home?"

The man looked at Neelix as if he were a small bug. "I'm taking you to the Mean Time Control for this Period."

"Period?" Torres asked.

"Mean?" Neelix said. He turned to Kim. "I don't like the sound of this."

The man made a small harrumphing sound, turned, and started to walk through the throng. He seemed to pay no attention to anyone else in the room, and none of the other travelers noticed him—or the away team—either.

Torres and Kim had to hurry to keep up with Neelix and the man. Neelix was tugging on the man's sleeve. "I sincerely think you should let us go on our way. Lieutenant Torres is well known for her right hook and—"

"Neelix!" Torres said.

"I'm simply letting him know that we can be mean as well. We don't control time, but we control other important things. We can be quite formidable." Neelix still clung to the man's sleeve. The man was staring down at him as if Neelix were little more than a child.

"I don't think he means angry-mean," Kim said in a loud whisper. "I think he means mean-mean."

"That's what I mean," Neelix said. "We can be mean-mean. We have B'Elanna here."

"He means—I mean—he—arg!" Torres interrupted herself. "Mean Time Control probably *refers* to the mathematical concept of average."

"Average?" Neelix said. "How can a Time Control be average?"

The man stopped and shook Neelix's hand off his sleeve. "The Mean Time Control handles problems outside of Real Time."

"Oh," Neelix said. "Well, that clarifies matters." He shook his head. But Torres was beginning to get a little clearer picture of what the man was talking about.

"You have clearly defined time periods, then?" she asked. "That's what you were referring to earlier when you mentioned the Time Control for this Period."

The man nodded. He weaved between members of a family. Torres hurried to catch up. Kim was right behind her. Neelix stared after the children, who were taller than he was, noted that the others were gone, and ran to rejoin the group.

"So how long is a period?" Torres asked.

"Five hundred thousand years," the man said, in a

tone that told her the passing children would have known this.

Torres wanted to stop walking. She felt as if she had almost grasped the concept the man was talking about. If they operated within periods, separated time into Real Time and Mean Time, then—

"Real Time runs forward for you, just like it does for us, then."

"Time always runs forward, ma'am. Sometimes we just travel backward."

She hated that tone. One of her professors at the academy used that tone with her. It made her feel . . . well, mean.

She glanced at Neelix. She would not prove him right within one hour of landing in this strange place.

"I still don't understand why you need to bring us to the Time Control."

"Probably because we're strangers," Kim said. He shot her a glance that let her know how uncomfortable he felt. She appreciated his feelings. She was uncomfortable too. But her way was to confront. His was to go along.

Her way was the only one that would get them answers.

"The Mean Time Control regulates travel," the man said, as if that were answer enough.

"I got that," Torres said. "We didn't intend to take the ship. We'll return it. It's a simple case of letting us go back."

"You cannot go back."

"Actually," Neelix said, "we could. We could just

get on the ship, I could sit down for a nap like I did before, the lights would go on, and—"

"No," the man said. "It's against the law."

"What?" Torres said. "What law?"

"I told you," the man said. "Control Ordinance 852.61."

"Which regulates what?" Torres asked.

"Intraperiod travel."

"If you don't travel between Periods, then how do you time travel?" Kim asked.

"*Intra*period," Torres said. "You can't travel within a single Period, can you?" That question was pointed at the guard. "Because if you do, you'll screw up Real Time. That's why you people let time run forward. You live out your lives within a Period, then—"

"No, ma'am. We may visit any Period we want, any Black Period that is. Red Periods are, of course, forbidden."

"Of course," Neelix said, sotto voce.

"Neelix!" Torres said, then she turned to the guard. "But you can't travel within the same Period. That's how you avoid paradox. This is fascinating."

"I wish I could study it in my room. In my bathtub," Neelix said. "Under sudsy hot water. Steaming, sudsy hot water—"

Kim jabbed Neelix and Neelix stopped talking.

Torres took the man's arm. His orange suit felt crinkly, like fresh paper. "Listen, we didn't purposefully break your laws. Your ship brought us here. We're willing to go back. In fact, we want to go back. The more you drag us around this Period, the more we could affect something."

"That may very well be," the man said. "Control will sort it out." He stopped in front of a booth and punched in a code. Then he swept a hand forward, indicating that Torres should step through.

She shook her head. "I don't think so," she said. "I think we'd better remain with the ship we arrived in. We have to get back into the future and—"

"Not without permission," the man in orange said, almost a touch of panic in his voice. "You have already time-jumped inside a Period without permission and that is a very serious offense."

Torres glanced around at the small, curious crowd that was now starting to form. And the man's accusations about time-jumping without permission sent an uneasy stir through the crowd.

"That was an accident," Torres said. "Your shuttle kidnapped us, not the other way around."

"That will be for Mean Time Control to figure out. Now, please." Again, he moved his hand in that curious, courtly gesture, as if he were trying to sweep Torres onto a dance floor.

She glanced at Kim and then at Neelix. What was she supposed to do? Leave the place and the ship that brought them from the future and put her hands in some unknown "Control"? A Mean Control? As Neelix said, it didn't sound promising.

She nodded to Kim and then turned to the man in orange. "I think we'll just go back to the shuttle that we came in. If you want to talk to us, we will be there. We have a spaceship in orbit around this planet three hundred thousand years in the future and our only goal is to return to it. We have no desire to cause problems. Understood?"

The man in orange just stood there staring at them with a panicked look.

"Let's go," Torres said. With more confidence than she felt, she started back across the huge room, Kim on her left and Neelix on her right, his short legs pumping hard to keep up with her stride.

"Halt now before I have to send a Time Breach alarm," the man in orange said forcefully. His words sent out a gasp through the large crowd that had now formed to watch the show.

"Phasers on stun," Torres said softly to Kim while not slowing down. "Make it back to that ship and hold it secure. Understood?"

"Understood," he said.

"Now!" Torres said and broke into a run for the door, her phaser in her hand. People scattered out of their way as a soft chiming echoed through the huge room.

She burst through the door and was immediately surrounded by a hundred orange-suited people, who were apparently expecting them. They held long-barreled weapons with the ends trained on her. Kim was surrounded by another large group, and so was Neelix.

"I thought you said intraperiod travel is forbidden," she said.

"You committed a Time Breach," the initial guard responded from behind her.

Torres stopped and slowly raised her hands, letting

her phaser drop to the ground. Kim did the same beside her.

"That was fast," Neelix said.

"I doubt we ever had a real chance," Torres said. Once these people had known Torres's plan, they had traveled back just far enough in time to prevent her and her team from getting to the shuttle.

Behind them their original guard said, "Now would you please come with me? You are in a great deal of trouble."

"Obviously," Neelix said.

Slowly Torres lowered her hands and followed the guard back across the room to the transporter booth. Her chances of seeing *Voyager* again had just gotten much, much worse.

# CHAPTER
# 6

KJANDERS LEANED AGAINST THE WALL IN THE TRANSPORT
Station. The grease from decades of travel was rub-
bing off on his bright blue tunic. He didn't care. The
thing was a disguise anyway. Better to look like a
bureaucrat heading for work in Period 18 than to wear
leisure clothes from Period 899. He hated this Period,
probably because it was his home Period. It offered no
room for growth or change, and he needed both.

He needed adventure. The Seconds-Watchers in
Control had no idea what adventure was. To them
adventure occurred whenever a shuttle took off.

But he had been to a hundred Periods before they
took his travel license away and he had used up
opportunities in every one of them. What he really
wanted to do was see something other than this
planet. He had heard of Planet-Hoppers before and

had thought of them often, especially when he traveled to dark times and stared at the stars above. Were all those worlds different from his own? Did they have warm and cool periods, ice ages, and forested ages, creatures that developed through time, and creatures that disappeared as the millennium passed? Or were they just like this place, the same yet different depending on where in the time line a traveler landed?

He would have loved to have asked the Planet-Hoppers that Control had picked up, but those three odd-looking people were doomed.

They had been doomed the moment they tried to make a break for it. They didn't seem to understand that making a straight run for it was the wrong way to avoid the orange suits. Causing a Time Alarm was a sure way to get executed real quick. He sighed. At least they were having an adventure.

He was just observing.

Then he stood up as an idea hit him.

Their bad luck just might have been his good luck. He'd been planning to take a shuttle, even though his license was gone. He had just needed a destination not guarded by the Watchmen. He had been lurking in this Transport Station for two days, trying to discover a place that he could disappear into, one that no other Time-Jumper had tried before.

Then these Planet-Hoppers had shown up.

Three hundred thousand years, the pretty woman with the ridged forehead had said. They had a ship, a planet-hopping ship, in orbit.

After the room was totally clear of the orange suits, he moved slowly toward the door they had entered.

This would be a perfect escape. He had managed to avoid Control so far. All they had managed was to rescind his license. They hadn't found him, just traces of him. His usual contacts could no longer help. He had stolen too much merchandise and brought it to the wrong Period. He was wanted, not just for the thefts, but also for hijacking a control ship and jumping within a Period. *That* had turned out unpleasant, but at least it had provided him with a quick escape. He had jumped a few years away, and then allowed the Control ship to return. Control had thought he stayed in the past, never thinking he would return to his own Real Time present.

It had seemed like a good idea then.

Two Real Time weeks later, the idea seemed a little lamebrained. Without help, he had had nowhere to go.

Until now.

He ambled through the door onto the warm concrete of the field and glanced around. It took him a moment before he spotted the Planet-Hoppers' shuttle. The shuttle seemed much older than the rest. It looked so bad that he was surprised it had been able to make the jump.

The shuttle sat on a pad that belonged to a different shuttle. When that shuttle returned, the automatic homing device of the old ship would take it back to the future, to the time of the Planet-Hoppers' Vacuum Ship.

And if his plan worked, it would soon be his Vacuum Ship.

* * *

Torres clenched her fists and held them at her side, battle-ready, as she stepped into the transporter. The dislocating change—something she would never completely get used to—occurred in a split second. One moment she was in the big transporter hall, the next she was in a room dug out of solid rock.

Neelix appeared beside her, eyes closed and body tilted backward as if he had been pushed. Once he materialized, he fell back against the clear walls of the transporter.

Kim appeared a moment after that, his dark eyes wide. He stood in full military posture, looking more like a Starfleet officer than Torres had ever seen him. Then she realized that he had dealt with their imprisonment with the Ocampa the same way; she just hadn't realized that his reserve had military components. Of course, then she had not been thinking, she had been reacting.

Here she was thinking.

And wondering why the three of them were such a spectacle.

The room's inhabitants stood around the transporter, five deep, staring at Torres, Kim, and Neelix. The stone room was hotter than the communal deserts on Hafir Minor, but that didn't stop the small crowd from wearing three layers of clothing—all black with white trim—collars up to their chins, sleeves that buttoned around their wrists, and leggings that tied below the ankle. Torres had noted a few people wearing these outfits in the great hall, but she had never noticed the shoes before.

The shoes were frivolous—they were sandals made

of the same clear material as the transporter walls, only the clear material had been treated with a black stain. The bottom of the shoes came to points beneath the toe and the heel, and required a tremendous amount of balance for the wearer to stand upright. Those shoes had to add at least six centimeters of height to the wearer—and gave a tremendous advantage to anyone trying to run away from these odd folks, as long as the person running away was wearing sensible shoes.

Torres made note of the clothing in the second after she materialized. Then she looked beyond the people to the room itself. The room had no doors, although an entire wall seemed to be missing on the far side. Computer stations were scattered around tiny pine trees that grew out of the dirt that composed the floor. Only a few chairs existed at all. Torres suddenly felt sympathy for all these workers. They wore those shoes, and spent all day on their feet.

Toward the open wall the trees changed from pine to a variety that Torres had never seen before. The broad leaves and ribbed bark made the trees look tropical. They disappeared into the opening leading somewhere. But since she didn't know where she was, and since these people could anticipate her every move, she couldn't make a run for it yet.

Their guard materialized beside her.

"Thank goodness," Neelix said, the human expression sounding natural on his lips. "I thought for a moment we would be abandoned to the whims of fate."

Both Torres and Kim shot him warning glances, which he seemed to ignore.

"After all," Neelix said to the small crowd before them, "you good people would never treat guests the way your orange-suited colleague does. He doesn't say hello, which I grant you is not custom in every culture, but it does, in most, signify politeness. He arrests visitors, and he makes up rules as he goes along. I ask you, is that any way to make people feel welcome?"

"Neelix," Torres hissed.

No one else answered him. Their guard stepped out of the transporter as if he hadn't heard Neelix at all. He pushed his way through the crowd—Torres was amazed that no one toppled over on those shoes—and then stopped at the open wall.

"I would advise you to follow me," he said.

"Where are we going?" Torres asked.

"To Control," he said.

"I thought this was Control," Torres said.

"They don't look mean enough," Neelix whispered.

"I don't know," Kim said. "Those shoes—"

"Ensign!" Torres said. The last thing she wanted was for Kim to pick up Neelix's bad habits.

"This is not Control. This is merely a stop along the way," the guard said. "Come along."

Torres glanced at her companions, giving them a silent order to follow her, then led the way through the crowd. A few people brushed against her, not too accidentally, she suspected. A few others made eye contact.

"Very few people go to Control," one of the women said, her voice hushed.

"Lucky us," Torres said.

"Time Breaches are serious," a man said.

"It's your fault," Neelix said. "If your ship hadn't taken us from our time, we would not be here. We would be peacefully minding our own business in that aban—"

The guard whirled and grabbed Neelix before he had a chance to finish his sentence. The guard held Neelix at eye level. "Your prattle takes risks of its own."

"I think," Kim said, "you might have been about to say something you shouldn't."

"I never say something I shouldn't," Neelix said.

The guard tightened his grip on Neelix's collar.

"Although," Neelix said, "I sometimes say things I regret."

The guard lowered him, then let go. "Now," the guard said. "Shut up and follow me."

Neelix bowed his head and followed, playing the contrite prisoner. Torres got out of the crowd. Once she did, she and Kim went through the open wall side by side.

The strange trees smelled of juniper and burning pitch. The odor was more pleasant than she had suspected it would be. The trees lined the wall, occasionally almost blocking doors. Orange suits came in and out of those doors, moving quickly and with purpose. A few people dressed in black tottered slowly by.

"Those shoes," Neelix said as he caught up to the guard. "Are they punishment for something?"

The guard squinted down at Neelix. "I told you to shut up."

"It was just a simple question," Neelix said.

"Actually," said another orange suit who had appeared beside Kim. "The shoes are a status symbol. The less you have to walk, the more ornate your shoes can be."

Torres wasn't certain she wanted to wear her jewelry on her feet. Of course, she wasn't that fond of baubles anyway. If something didn't have a purpose it didn't make much sense to her.

The orange suit walking beside Kim was a woman, slender to the point of gauntness, her hair long and caught in an orange thong behind her neck. More of the orange suits who had come out of the doors had joined their little party until Torres felt like part of an invasion force going through tunnels in Cardassia.

Finally the wide corridor forked and opened into another stone room. The trees disappeared completely, and it took a few extra steps before their pungent odor disappeared from Torres's nostrils.

This room reminded Torres more of a shuttlebay. It was wide and tall and the stone had a flat, utilitarian feel. Although the floor was long and flat, and not composed of dirt, but of more of that concrete material, it was empty except for one ship that sat in the very center.

The ship was a miniature version of the shuttle they had arrived in. It lacked the long landing legs, and the ramp went in a side instead of under it. The ship's circumference was also much smaller. She doubted a hundred people could fit inside.

She stopped when she reached the cement floor. "I hope," she said in her calmest voice, "that this ship will take us back to our own time."

"It would be so wonderful," Neelix said. "I have to tell you that I much prefer newer ships. They are ever so much more reliable. You can escort us back, meet my darling Kes, and then be on your way. I can guarantee that we will be on ours. It would be no inconvenience to any of us and—"

"This is the way to Control," the first guard said.

"I don't believe that taking a shuttle anywhere except three hundred thousand years in the future will help us," Torres said. She wished for Tuvok. Her calm was slipping.

"We are not trying to help you," the first guard said. "You committed a Time Breach."

"We had no idea that your ship would bring us here. Your homing device was set for this time. It's the ship's problem, not ours," Torres said. "Just take us home. We promise we'll never come here again."

The woman beside Kim suddenly grabbed his arm.

"Hey!" he said. "I hadn't even made my move yet."

Torres looked at him. "It wouldn't have done any good, Ensign," she said. "Even if they let us take that shuttle, we probably couldn't run it. It looks like a different model from the one that brought us."

"Control is expecting you," the first guard said.

"Well, they can wait a minute," Torres said. "If we decide to go, you can always back up the time stream a little."

All the orange suits gasped around her. They had

that shocked look that most Starfleet officers had when someone slandered the Academy.

"I suppose I said something wrong," she said.

"You violated Ordinance 661.33," the first guard said.

"Fortunately," said the woman beside Kim, "the six-hundred series are all misdemeanors."

"We could," the first guard said to the woman, "attribute this to stress and overlook it."

She nodded. "But let's see how the interview with Control goes. You know they hate speech crimes. And overlooking a misdemeanor can itself be worthy of a fine. The new twelve-hundred series Ordinances . . ."

"Is everything numerical to these people?" Neelix asked Kim. "My mind spins from the math."

". . . demand constant vigilance on the part of . . ."

"There hasn't been any real math yet," Kim said.

". . . documentation is enormous . . ."

"Except the actual time travel itself," Neelix said. "Have you any real comprehension of three hundred thousand? I once scavenged three hundred thousand lisern seeds off a Uteke freighter, and they filled my cargo bay to the brim. It took me a week to count the things."

". . . therefore," the woman concluded, "we should make note of the violation."

Torres rolled her eyes. Didn't anyone else understand the seriousness of this? "I think we should do as they say and shut up," Torres said to Kim and Neelix.

"That's good," said a third guard, the one who had stayed close to Torres, "because actually my colleagues are wrong. Ordinance 661.33 governs time judgments often made in jest. To suggest a crime to more than three others, however, especially to Time Patrol officers, falls in the four-hundred series, most applicable 412.11. Of course, we could add 486.90, which includes incitement to riot—"

"Enough!" Torres said. "Just take us on your damn shuttle."

The orange suits looked at each other. None of them moved. The woman beside Kim said, "Are we to treat them like four-hundred series violators, eight-hundred series violators, or six-hundred series violators?"

"I think we should let Control decide that," the first guard said.

"Excuse me," Kim said.

Everyone looked at him, including Neelix, who appeared to be holding his breath.

"But none of you could help us even if you wanted to, could you?"

"We have jurisdiction for six-hundred-level crimes," the woman said archly.

"We do decide who goes to Control and who doesn't," the first guard said.

"What I'm asking is—" Kim glanced at Torres. She could see the wild panic in his eyes. "—do any of you have the authority to send us back to our own time?"

"Absolutely not!"

"No!"

"And who would want it?"

The first two responses were chorused in unison by

most of the orange suits. Only the woman answered differently.

"I thought you were due for promotion to Control," the first guard said softly to her.

She shook her head. "I withdrew my application."

"But the increase in pay would be spectacular," another suit said.

"It's not enough," the woman said. "Do you know that you would be outside Periods for much of your career and that some Control are even asked to forgo families and . . ."

"Can we leave?" Torres asked.

". . . if I were to explain that, I would commit a six-hundred violation myself, but suffice to say . . ."

"Hey!" Torres said, louder than before. "Can we go?"

". . . I think double the amount of money they pay us still wouldn't be worth the hassles . . ."

"Do I have to commit another four-hundred-level violation?" Torres said as loudly as she could without shouting.

That shut them up. They looked at her. The woman's mouth was hanging open.

"I would like to go see your Control people," Torres said. "That's where we were going before we got sidetracked. Can we get on with this?"

"Certainly," the first guard said, somewhat chagrined.

He led them up the ramp. Kim brushed close to Torres. "What were you doing?" he whispered.

"You were right. They're just petty officials. Let's go somewhere where something can get done."

"Bravo!" Neelix said.

The ramp leveled into the ship itself. Torres had been right. This ship was much smaller on the inside. It had only ten seats in a circle around the wall, and six orange guards came along, including the original but not (thank heaven) the gossipy woman. The first guard gave Kim, Torres, and Neelix the seats in the middle. The six guards faced them, as the door slammed closed.

The seats were soft, but not too soft. Torres squirmed, trying to get comfortable, when the little ship shook slightly and seemed to lift, then settled almost as quickly back to the deck.

Torres's heart felt as if it had jumped into her throat. She swallowed hard. Calm, she repeated to herself. Calm. She tried to imagine Tuvok in this situation, and tried to imitate him.

"So tell me," Torres said as if the answer didn't matter to her at all, "how many years did we just travel through time?"

The lead orange guard stood. "Exactly four hundred and forty-four million, five hundred thousand years."

Torres felt her head spin and she took a deep breath. "What?"

The door hissed open.

"How many zeros is that?" Neelix asked Kim.

Kim shook his head.

Neelix extended his right hand, counted his fingers several times using the thumb and forefinger of his left hand, and then looked up at Torres. All the charm had left his features, and for the first time since she had known him, his cheek hair stood out straight, and the spots on his skin looked livid.

"I think," he said, "I finally understand how you and the other members of *Voyager* must feel being so far from home."

# CHAPTER
# 7

THE COUPLE GOING UP THE RAMP HAD THREE CHILDREN AND four times the maximum luggage for a warm-climate period. Drickel waited at the bottom of the ramp while the family separated the pieces of luggage, cheap mesh bags that would split apart before their trip was over. The mother ran down the ramp, carrying six bags to the transport, apologizing to the other passengers as she went. She dialed in her personal code, got it wrong, cursed, and redialed. When the bags disappeared, she ran back up the ramp, apologizing again, and then rejoined her family. Security, which watched for precisely that kind of violation, waved the rest of the passengers through.

The shuttle was crowded although all the passengers had seats. Drickel leaned back in his chair, arms and legs crossed. Only a few people looked at his utilitari-

an uniform. They assumed, because his footwear was practical and his clothing drab, that he was a low-level bureaucrat. If they had thought about it, they would have realized that he had one of the more exciting jobs in the system.

But people rarely thought of that. The chances of running into the same person again were slim. So for the most part everyone ignored everyone else.

The shuttle lifted and settled twice before Drickel's stop, but only a handful of people—most of them in orange jumpsuits—got off. He was heading for the main shuttle station of Period 889. Most of the people had got off up-line in times much more conducive to family travel.

He traveled the millions of years with his eyes closed. Even though he hadn't been on the shuttle in six-point-seven Real Time years, every movement of the shuttle was familiar to him. He could almost plot the course in his sleep.

When the shuttle landed in 889, Drickel disembarked alone. It didn't surprise him. No one had ever gotten off the shuttle in this Period with him, not in all the Real Time years he'd been a Watchman.

As he walked down the ramp, he remembered why he disliked this station. He hated the air here. It was far too dry. It would be even worse where he was going. His nose always dried up and it was everything he could do to keep enough balm on his lips to keep them from bleeding.

His job consisted of answering calls and guarding the abandoned shuttle stations in fifty different Periods. The choice Periods, of course, rarely required his services. He always traveled to the difficult Periods, the one no one wanted to visit, not even on a scholarly quest.

Eight-eighty-nine Real Time was tolerable, but three hundred thousand years farther along wasn't.

As he stepped off the ramp the air instantly dried out his nose and eyes. It was a warm afternoon, closer to hot on the paved surface, and it made him long for his jungle. There the air was moist. It hugged him like steam and felt like a friendly presence. Here the air was an enemy, taking his life forces and giving him nothing in return.

He stopped to allow himself to adjust to people again. They flowed around him like water around a stone. Most wore the blues and purples of government workers, but a few tottered by on their pointed platform shoes, expressing their distaste at public transportation.

Most of these folks were middle-income bureaucrats who earned just enough money to look as if they earned more. The really important people were invisible to most of the citizens. They never felt as if they had to wear clothing to impress, never spent ostentatiously in public. Drickel liked to think of himself as one of them—his home was the place all of his earnings went—but in actuality, he was just one step above the tottering middle management. The difference between him and them was simply one of information. They knew what the future would bring.

He had been there.

Repeatedly.

The crowds always made him a bit dizzy. He made

himself breathe the dry air and watched people pass.
He was lucky that he had been called to 889. The
really popular periods had stations three times this
busy. Many of these shuttles took off less than a
quarter full. It didn't surprise him. He couldn't imagine why anyone would visit this time period, let alone
live here. But obviously millions did.

He walked slowly through the heat and dry air to
the nearest transport building, letting the small
crowds move around him. He had learned years ago
that being in a hurry just never did much good,
especially in this job.

He entered the building, wincing when he realized
the air was warmer here, but smelled worse. People
stepped in and out of the transporters, the faces
changing, but the movements staying the same. Con-
versations flowed like good music, punctuated by loud
and silent moments. He walked around a line and
went to a booth that appeared to be out of order. It
was actually reserved for service personnel. On the
destination pad he keyed in his special code and then
stepped inside.

The noise of the talking crowds in the terminal
disappeared in midthrum. He had a moment of
silence before he heard the hum of machines and the
clicking of keys. The transporter had moved him
almost a kilometer below the surface of the shuttle
field.

He blinked in surprise. All of the bureaucrats were
away from their computers. Most were sipping black-
bean sugar water from pointed glass cups that
matched their shoes. They were all speaking in soft,

animated voices. The bureaucrats' high collars and tight sleeves reminded him of the rules they all enforced: restrictive and necessary only because others might take advantage.

He stepped off the pad into the high-ceilinged room that smelled of pine. He had always thought of that as cool air scent, but someone had decided to fill this hot stuffy office with baby trees. Farther down one hall stood Aleisen trees, and even farther, ferns grew out of the stone. Computers winked at various locations near the trees, and the few chairs in the room were occupied.

This was Shuttle Control for Period 889 and the connection to Mean Time Control in Period One. The two hundred employees down here were in charge of making sure a ship went only to the exact point and time it was programmed to go. This control room, and the others like it in every Period, were the very soul and heart of the society spread out through almost a billion years of time.

Drickel liked this control room more than any of the other Periods he worked in. He liked the plants and the warm feel. The people here had made this place comfortable and welcoming. Some Controls had done nothing more than leave the rock walls the chambers were carved out of and stick in desks. Those always seemed dark, oppressive, and cold to him. He couldn't imagine how anyone could work there.

"Hey, Drickel, it's been a lot of Real Time." A heavyset man wearing a meter-tall red wig set his black-bean sugar water glass in the dirt beside a pine and extended his hand.

"About thirteen years, Red." Drickel switched his carryall bag to his other hand and stepped forward, grasping Red's firm grasp. He had forgotten how his name sounded when spoken by another person. And Red was one of his favorites. He got his name from the red wigs he had favored since he was a boy. "You're looking young. Still living in One with all the masses?"

Red laughed. "Wow, what a memory. Actually when they promoted me, I moved to Eight-Seven. Got myself a place down in Southern City. Still crowded, but not as bad as One."

"You really should try the wilderness life," Drickel said. He missed it already.

"My wife's been telling me the same thing. Who knows." Red shrugged and then glanced around. "You just missed all the excitement. We actually had a Time Alarm right above us this morning."

"You're kidding," Drickel said. He hadn't heard of a Time Alarm in all his years of service. No wonder no one was working. This would be a real day to remember. "What happened?"

"Amazing violations," Red said. "Four last I heard."

"Four people?"

"Nope," Red said. "Four violations before they got shipped to Control. One an eight-hundred level."

Drickel felt a chill run down his back. Eight-hundreds were extremely serious. "Actual physical violation?" he asked.

"More than one, if you want to get technical," Red said. His normally placid eyes had a slight glint.

Shuttle Control never saw much excitement. "Three Planet-Hoppers tried to steal a Period shuttle. We back-timed a force of sixty to stop them. Control whisked the prisoners through here and back to One without much delay."

"Enough delay to cause two more four-hundred violations!" someone yelled from the back. Clearly the group had been discussing the event ever since it happened.

Drickel shook his head in amazement. Back-timing was seldom used and very dangerous. Control must have thought the situation drastic. He wondered if he would ever discover the details. He doubted it. So he moved through the scattered groups, shaking his head when a man offered him a glass, and headed for the tunnel.

Red kept pace with him. They weren't really friends, but they might have been if Drickel had been the friendly type.

"What brings you back to good old Eight-eighty-nine?" Red asked.

"A problem up-Period they want my help on."

Red glanced around to make sure no one was listening. "I've got clearance now for up-time. I'll walk you." They started off toward the back of the big room, following a path that led in and around desks and trees.

"The promotion got you into the Back Room, huh?" The Back Room was the high-security part of Control. It was the branch of Control he worked for. Only a very few people in each Period knew the truth about the future in Real Time. That was one of the many reasons why it was so forbidden to travel inside any 500,000-year Period. If knowledge of the Near Future got out, it would destroy the society.

"Yeah," Red said, shaking his head. "Sometimes I wish they'd never told me all the future-history stuff. I would sleep better, you know?"

Drickel knew. But he had done enough work up-time to stop fearing the Near Future. Now he just complained about it—to himself, since he was not allowed to discuss his work with anyone outside of the Back Room.

Red stopped at a plain door labeled NO ADMITTANCE and keyed a code into the panel. Then he put his hand on a plate and a small light flashed orange. Drickel moved forward and repeated the procedure. As the light flashed again, the door opened and the two men moved inside.

In front of them stretched a long stone hallway with no decoration. The air here had a processed chill. Drickel shuddered as he always did when he stepped into the Back Room.

"You been up-Period at all?" he asked as they headed down the hall.

Red nodded. "Just once, right after the Second Exodus. I have nightmares about the emptiness."

Drickel nodded. "I'm jumping about fifty thousand years after that. I've been there a few times. Most everything is totally gone except for the old ships. Planet-Hoppers mess with those ships. I'm getting real tired of that."

"Anyone living there at all?" Red asked.

"No," Drickel said as they reached the end of the

tunnel and another thick door opened. "Too damn cold and dry. The entire planet is deserted during that time."

"Amazing," Red said.

"Not really. Everyone left during the Second Exodus and they shut down all of the Period shuttles." Drickel glanced at Red. He'd seen Red's reaction before, had had the same reaction himself. The only difference was that Drickel had had a lot of empty Real Time to think about the choices.

"I mean, Red, think about it," Drickel said. "Now we can live anywhere in time and some Periods are too damn crowded. But if we could live in that same Period without people, most of us would. The dimensional shifts must have seemed like a miracle when they were discovered. Over two and a half million choices of an uninhabited planet per Period. If you had that kind of choice, wouldn't you go and live in a dimension that was not crowded? Or maybe totally empty? Imagine having an entire planet to yourself."

"My mind can't grasp other dimensions, let alone two and a half million of them," Red said. "I keep thinking, what if one of my kids made a dimension shift without telling me? How would I ever find him?"

"Control would," Drickel said, although he wasn't so certain. "That's what we're here for."

"Good point," Red said. But Drickel could tell that Red didn't believe it any more than he did.

The operator on duty was a woman who had sensibly abandoned her high button collars and tight sleeves. She still wore tied leggings, but on her small feet the pointed platforms looked stunning. She smiled at Drickel when he introduced himself. Her name was Noughi, and if he hadn't been responding to an Alarm, he might have spent a few precious Real Time minutes getting to know her.

She worked alone in a small, stone-walled room that smelled of high-density sugar water. A single drooping fern covered half of her desk. Behind her, a large Control station filled one wall, and the other wall was filled with a small sledlike device with a padded bench seat in it. A personal time-jump shuttle.

"I got another reading just before you arrived," Noughi said. "On this station. But it's a bit of a distance from the time-jump point."

Drickel nodded. Those Planet-Hoppers were really eager. Sometimes there would be several trigger events after the first Alarm. "How late will I be in Real Time?"

"The time-jump point is an hour after the first alarm. I tried to get dispensation to send you in earlier, but Control says no to that for some reason."

Always regulations to worry about. And other things. "Is the underground shuttle still being maintained in that time?" he asked.

Noughi shook her head. "Not a chance. But the tunnels are mostly still open. You got a personal transporter in case of a cave-in?"

Drickel tapped his belt and held up his bag. "Got all my standard tricks."

"Sounds like you're in for a hike," Red said.

"Makes me earn my pay." Drickel turned back to Noughi. "What's the source of the interference?"

"We're not sure," she said, "but we think there's a

Vacuum Ship in orbit over this station at the point you are jumping in. They may have sensors, so stay out of phase."

Drickel nodded. "Well then, it's time I go scare them away." He tossed his bag on the orange chair, then sat beside it. He grinned at Noughi. "Anything else I should know?"

"Just my Real Time address," she said. "I'll code it into your files."

"If it's anywhere crowded, you'll have to visit him," Red said.

Her smile was warm. "All he has to do is ask."

Drickel smiled in return. He would ask—after he checked her files. The open collar was intriguing but the shoes hinted at some values he didn't hold. He waved his hand. She nodded and pressed a panel on her board.

The next thing he knew he was in blackness.

He swore softly to himself as he fumbled around on his belt. After so many years in the business, it was amazing that he never remembered to turn on a lamp before he jumped.

Kjanders attached himself to three different family groups near the old shuttle, trying to pretend as if he belonged. If one of the parents looked at him, he would move on. The key was to look involved, but not too involved. He managed to keep himself near the shuttle and no orange suit had even noticed him.

Not yet anyway.

He was only about ten meters away from the shuttle when he heard it whir. A burst of excitement ran through him. He sprinted across the pavement and managed to get up the ramp as it was rising.

He slipped into one of the seats as the door snapped shut.

The lights went on, and the whirring continued. This old thing sounded as if it would fall apart at any second.

He clung to the seat edge, the thick old padding separating under the pressure of his fingers. The hardest part was over. He was jumping three hundred thousand years to where a Planet-Hopper ship was waiting. He'd get lost in the crowds and then figure out a way onto the Planet-Hopper ship.

The old ship lifted, then settled back down with a soft thump. He got out of his seat, picking bits of stuffing from his nails. If he got away from this ship, Control would never find him. He would be completely free. He stood beside the door ready to amble slowly down the ramp as if he belonged there. The door opened and the blast of cold, dry air hit him.

He pulled his collar shut and moved forward.

The howl of a wind greeted him, blowing dust and sand into his eyes. He wiped his face, unease settling in his stomach. Normally, he heard the whir of ships, the dull murmur of conversation even before he stepped out the door.

Here only the wind greeted him.

They must have found a way to dampen sound. He walked down the ramp, and stopped halfway.

There were no people.

The transport buildings were nothing more than piles of rubble.

All the shuttles were parked in place.

And most of them were obviously too broken-down to ever be used.

He was trapped in a future he didn't recognize.

He glanced up, looking for the Planet-Hoppers' ship, but he saw nothing above him except the gray overcast sky.

# CHAPTER

# 8

CAPTAIN JANEWAY CIRCLED AROUND THE BRIDGE ONCE, wishing she had more room to walk, to think. When she reached the captain's chair, she sat down and turned her own armchair console toward her.

"Mr. Tuvok," she said, "I want you to maintain a lock on that humanoid. I want to know each time he takes a breath. Mr. Paris, I want you to scan for any anomalies in the area. Chakotay, see if you can find our away team underground, aboveground, or floating in the atmosphere. I want answers, people."

She manipulated her console for answers on her own. The short flight of the ship disturbed her. She suspected that the ship was a mask for some other kind of transportation. Perhaps its small motion triggered a transporter or opened a hole underground.

"Captain," Tukov said, "the humanoid has left the ship and is standing on the ramp. I do not know what its intentions are, nor do I know what kind of creature it is. It appears to be male, six feet, four inches tall, and not that significantly different from other humanoids. It does have eight digits on each hand. I would suspect that it has eight toes per foot as well."

"Keep me apprised, Mr. Tuvok," Janeway said. At the moment she didn't care if the man below had eight fingers or eighty-five. She was just hoping he would lead her to her crew members.

"There are underground caverns, Captain," Chakotay said, "but they're in ruins. None of them provide a clear path to the surface. I've scanned them and found no life-forms. I suspect those underground caverns were once part of this society and collapsed over time."

Janeway had already come to that conclusion on her own. The ships on the surface were also empty. As far as her sensors showed, the single humanoid male who had arrived in the ship was the only living creature on Alcawell.

"Captain," Paris said, a touch of excitement in his voice, "there are trace elements of chroniton particles around that ship."

"Are you sure, Mr. Paris?"

"Certain," he said. "They've slipped back in time."

"How do you know that?" Janeway asked.

"It's their turn."

Janeway ignored that last. She examined the small area near the ship with her console's sensors. The elements were there, but tiny. "Time travel? Mr. Tuvok, is that logical? If this culture could travel in time, then why would everything be in ruins?"

"Uncertain, Captain. We do not have enough data."

"Is it possible?" Janeway asked.

"Quite, Captain," Tuvok said. "Although we must rule out several possibilities, such as if the chroniton particles came from a source other than the ship itself."

"Time travel would explain how that humanoid arrived in their ship so quickly," Paris said.

"Chakotay," Janeway said. "Any sign of our people?"

"None," Chakotay said. "Not even trace signatures. They haven't been beamed anywhere and there are no other anomalies out there."

"Mr. Tuvok, is our friend moving?"

"No, Captain. He has reached the base of the ramp and remained there."

"Good." Janeway returned her console to its usual position. She stood, touched her hair to make sure all the strands were in place, and made a deep resigned sigh. "Mr. Tuvok, get a transporter lock on our friend and beam him to security. Then join me there. I want you to accompany us as well, Chakotay. Mr. Paris, you have the bridge."

She headed for the turbolift. That passenger would have answers. He would have to.

One minute he was standing on the deserted station, the next he was in a room done mostly in grays.

A bunk was attached to the wall. Three walls surrounded him. The room looked out on a large open area. More smaller rooms surrounded it.

Kjanders appreciated the warmth. He hadn't dressed for the chill of the planet.

He sat on the bunk with a sigh. Somehow the Planet-Hoppers had transported him. Or someone had. Even though they weren't using booths, the feeling was the same, just slower.

He only hoped he hadn't been caught by Control.

The bunk was a bit short for his large frame. Sitting on the edge brought his knees almost to his chest level. The mattress was soft, though, and covered with a blanket made from a material he didn't recognize. The colors in the area were mostly grays and silvers, dull colors that belonged only in institutions.

They were leaving him alone here. He would have to find where to go on his own. He got up and walked to the center of the room. As he passed the two walls, a hot forcefield slapped his body. The field appeared only when he touched it.

A prisoner.

Control had found him.

Then a door he hadn't even seen hissed open. A slender woman wearing a red and black uniform and two short men, one with dark skin and pointed ears, the other with a drawing on his forehead, hurried in. They all had small chins and wore their hair close to their skulls in a manner most unattractive (not even a tenth of a meter in height!). The red of their uniforms was dull and not even the dominant color.

He let out a small sigh of relief. They weren't

Control. He hadn't had to find the Planet-Hopper ship. It had found him.

The woman approached the forcefield. The two men flanked her.

Kjanders walked as close to the field as he could get and found himself looking down at all of them.

"I am Captain Kathryn Janeway of the Federation *Starship Voyager*. Who are you and what have you done with my crew?"

Kjanders gaped at her, then rethought his position. Somehow he had expected the Planet-Hoppers to be as glad to see him as he was to see them. But he was wrong. Of course he was wrong. He would have to convince them to let him stay.

"I'm Kjanders. I'm—an engineer on Alcawell, Period Eight-eighty-nine. I didn't do anything with your crew." The first lie came easily. He hoped he wouldn't have to do that too often.

"Period?" the man with the pointed ears asked.

"I suppose that's confusing, since this is still Period Eight-eighty-nine." Kjanders shook his head. "Although it doesn't seem that way."

"At the moment, I am more concerned about the three missing members of my crew," the woman said. "They were in the ship you arrived in moments before you."

He couldn't lie too much. He would never be able to keep everything straight. That's what got him in trouble in the first place. "A tall woman with a big forehead, a child-sized man with too much short hair, and a man who looks something like that one?" Kjanders nodded toward the man with the drawing.

"Something like," the woman said. Her voice was curt and businesslike.

"I saw them before I got trapped in the ship," Kjanders said. "They got off and I went to examine it. It was so old—"

"Off?" the woman snapped. "Off where?"

"Three hundred thousand years ago. Still Period Eight-eighty-nine, though. That was the problem. Control got them. I'm sorry."

"Control?" the woman said. "What is Control?"

"The Time Control," Kjanders said. "Your crew committed an eight-hundred violation. Control has to act in those cases."

"Three hundred *thousand* years?" the man with the drawing murmured.

"Explain this violation," the woman said, ignoring the man.

"They traveled intraperiod. Strictly forbidden. A felony, actually."

"If they traveled within a Period," the man with the strange ears said, "and you saw them and, as you say, that was Period Eight-eighty-nine, and this is Period Eight-eighty-nine, then you committed the same violation."

For Planet-Hoppers, these people were sharp. Kjanders nodded. "But it was accidental. I just wanted to examine the ship. I'd never seen one so old."

"It was accidental for them too," the woman said. "Surely your Control will know that."

"Control doesn't believe in accidents," Kjanders said. This wasn't going as well as he wanted. He had to shift their attention, and getting out of this prison might help. "Would you happen to have any food or drink? It has been some Real Time since I ate."

"Mr. Tuvok," the woman said, "weapons?"

The pointed-eared man shook his head. "Nothing that registers, Captain."

"All right," the woman said. She clasped her hands behind her back. "Mr. Kjanders, if we release you and take you to a communal area, I want your word that you will do nothing to us or our ship."

"I wouldn't," he said, with honest shock. "I certainly don't want to go back down to the planet. It's empty."

"That it is," the woman said. "I will leave you with Mr. Tuvok. He and security will take you to the officers' mess hall. Along the way I want you to figure out a way to explain the situation my crew is in, and ways that I can help them."

"You can't help them," Kjanders said. "They're with Control."

"Oh, I'll help them," the woman said. "The question is whether or not I do it with your cooperation." She turned to the man with the drawing. "Chakotay, you're with me."

Then she whirled and left, the man she called Chakotay following her. The Tuvok man remained. "You'd best cooperate with her," the Tuvok man said.

"I gathered that," Kjanders said. He took a deep breath. He had wanted adventure. And the adventure had definitely begun.

* * *

"Opinion, Commander?" Janeway asked as they stepped into the corridor.

"He's not lying about the trouble the away team is in," Chakotay said. "Three hundred *thousand* years. Captain, no starship has ever traveled back that far. We've been lucky to travel a few hundred years."

Janeway did not want to think about the actual time distance. That was a problem she would worry about later. "I know, Chakotay. But those ships obviously have the capability to travel. I just want to know how."

"If we show up and what he says about their laws is true, we'll be in the same kind of trouble that the away team is in."

"I realize that," Janeway said. She walked to the turbolift and ordered it to the correct floor. "I'll reserve judgment until I hear more about his people. What I want to know is your opinion of this man."

Chakotay stopped beside her in the lift. He gave her one of his deep, soulful looks. She braced herself. His opinions were always accurate, and always worthwhile. "He's lying. Not about the important things, but about himself. I did not like his answer to Tuvok's question about the law violation."

"I didn't either," Janeway said. "Is he dangerous?"

Chakotay frowned. "Not that I can tell. I can't imagine someone traveling purposefully in time to an abandoned station without a weapon or some means of protection. That lends credence to his accident statement. But the fact that he, as an engineer, would get on a ship that took off unexpectedly doesn't ring true."

"Exactly," Janeway said. The lift stopped and they got off. "Chakotay, I want you present while he eats. If you get a better sense of him, let me know. I don't want someone dangerous having free rein on my ship, but I also don't want to imprison someone unnecessarily."

Chakotay nodded.

"I will join you in a few minutes," Janeway said. "I'm going to get Carey to study those ships from here. Now that we know they can travel in time, I suspect figuring out how to use them will be easier. Perhaps we'll have a solution of our own without help from this Kjanders person."

"I hope so," Chakotay said. "Because I didn't like the sound of his 'Control.'"

By the time Janeway arrived in the officers' mess Kjanders was already eating. He had a glass of synthale before him and one of Neelix's dishes obviously prepared by someone Neelix had taught. Chakotay sat to one side of Kjanders, Tuvok to the other. A guard stood outside the door as well. If Kjanders wanted to try anything, he would have trouble accomplishing it.

"Captain," Kjanders said, waving a forkful of red and green glop at her. "Your friends Chakotay and Tuvok were explaining the structure of this ship. On Alcawell we have not had a military structure in many Periods, but we have a bureaucracy. They assure me that this system is more efficient."

"Tuvok." Janeway grinned at him as she sat down. "I thought Vulcans didn't lie."

"Captain," Tuvok said, "I firmly believe that the Starfleet system is designed—"

"I was kidding, Tuvok."

Tuvok glared at her. Over the time he had spent in human company he had grown accustomed to dry humor—had even practiced some of it himself—but when situations became tense he reverted to taking every statement literally.

Janeway folded her hands on the table. Kjanders's food smelled of Talaxian drige spice and broccoli. Her stomach growled. It had been a long time since she ate. It would probably be even longer until she got another chance. But she really didn't want to share any repast with a possible prisoner.

"No dinner, Captain?" Kjanders asked, eating the glop off his fork.

She shook her head. "Please continue. I didn't mean to interrupt."

"Well," Kjanders said, speaking around his food, "they were telling me about the ranking system here, and I was telling them about the bureaucracy, but I didn't mention how it came about. I was thinking that the best way to do what you asked, Captain, is to give you a brief history. Then, if I'm still not being clear, you could let me know and I could clarify as best I can."

"Fine," Janeway said. His history had better be short. She didn't want to spend precious time learning unimportant facts.

Kjanders took a sip of the synthale, swallowed, and smiled at her. Then he leaned back in his chair. "About two thousand Real Time years ago a team led by a man named Caxton discovered time travel. They learned very quickly that time lines could be changed with just the slightest of tampering. This tampering caused serious problems. So in those early years, a very small and powerful circle were the only people who even knew that we could travel in time."

"Was your culture traveling in space?" Tuvok asked.

"A bit," Kjanders said. "We were having trouble with population density. But Alcawellians, even then, tended to choose a site and live there as long as they could. They would defend that site to the death and have no real reason to leave it. Space travel seemed like a lot of effort to get somewhere no one wanted to go. Then, when the early ships exploded due to bad design, space travel lost its support."

"Tuvok," Janeway said, "I need information that might help get our people back. Your fascination with this culture is understandable, but right now I want no sidetracks. Continue, Mr. Kjanders."

Kjanders shot what appeared to be a nervous glance at Tuvok. "Well," Kjanders said, "Caxton and his friends in government finally decided that space was both unpopular and too dangerous, but the history of the planet was a wide-open playground. Alcawell is over nine billion years old. Over five billion of those years it has been capable of sustaining our needs. However, we only evolved on the planet during about a half million years or so."

"So people started going back in time?" Chakotay asked.

"Actually, they started living in time. Caxton and his team divided up the entire history of the planet, forward and back, into five-hundred-thousand-year chunks. Each five hundred thousand years is called a Period."

Janeway nodded. So that was the Period Kjanders had referred to when he arrived. And because the away team was three hundred thousand years in the past, they were still in the same Period.

"Our dating system is a bit confusing," Kjanders said, "since we did not alter our Real Time calendar when we discovered time travel. Instead, each Period follows a Real Time calendar based on our old calendar."

"When you refer to Real Time," Chakotay said, "you mean linear time. Right now, you are existing in Real Time."

"Exactly," Kjanders said. "We may travel hundreds of thousands or even millions of years, but we live a normal Real Time life span. Which, for us, is about a hundred years."

"Let me see if I understand this," Janeway said. "Each Period is five hundred thousand years long. The years within those five hundred thousand run chronologically. So year one in the first Period is five hundred thousand years away from year one in the second period."

"Exactly," Kjanders said. "The system is a bit confused because the first Periods were set up before Caxton and his people discovered that some Periods are bad no matter what. They designated those Periods as Red Periods. No one may travel to them. Even moving a stone in those Periods might change the course of history. But we travel in Black Periods, allowed Periods, where we can touch anything we want."

Tuvok templed his fingers and brought them to his lips, contemplating. "That effectively eliminates all time paradoxes then," he said. "I assume Red Periods cover Periods of important biological change. The Black Periods have a span long enough that if a person changes something in year one, Black Period One, it wouldn't matter in year one, Black Period Two."

"Right," Kjanders said.

Janeway had enough theory. She wanted something she could use to help Torres, Kim, and Neelix. "What is today's date as you people count it in Real Time?"

"I don't know exactly," Kjanders said. "As I mentioned, I didn't plan my trip here. I am guessing that it is about three hundred thousand, one hundred, give or take some years, Period Eight-eighty-nine."

Janeway nodded. "And where exactly are my people, in your Real Time years?"

"Three thousand seventy-one Real Time, Period Eight-eighty-nine. And that's their problem," Kjanders said. "They didn't jump far enough. Time-jumping within a Period is forbidden. The trip here is the first time I have ever done it."

"So your people are not allowed to see short-term futures," Tuvok said.

"Or the short-term past," Kjanders said.

"This is important?" Chakotay asked.

"It prevents fiscal speculation through time," Tuvok said. "It also prevents a person from killing his own grandfather and all the other standard time paradoxes. In other words, when these people get in ships, they only move at five-hundred-thousand-year jumps exactly."

"That seems quite important," Janeway said. "No wonder your people protect it so ferociously. What happens to someone who jumps inside a Period?"

"In school they used a metaphor to describe the ships. The metaphor is Caxton's and clearly dated, but it might work for you. Since he belonged to a society that looked at Planet-Hopping—"

"Planet-Hopping?" Chakotay asked.

Kjanders shrugged. "That's what your form of travel is called. It's not very well understood anymore."

Janeway suppressed a sigh. She understood her officers' fascination—she shared it—but the more she discovered from Kjanders, the more she understood what deep trouble her away team was in. "Continue, Mr. Kjanders."

"Oh, yes. As I was saying, since his society is similar to yours you might appreciate his description. He said each ship is set to run on rails between time Periods. There are no rails, of course, but he was trying to explain the new form of travel to a culture that rode on rails to a prescribed destination every day."

No physical rails. Janeway stored that knowledge for Carey. But some sort of predetermined destination system existed.

"Since each ship is set to run a strict line between time Periods, travel inside a single Period is very, very rare and only possible by Control." Kjanders glanced around at his three-member audience and then focused again on Janeway. "I haven't heard of anyone doing it in my lifetime, but I do know that the punishment is death. I'm sorry."

"Death!" Janeway said. She had had a feeling about this.

"That would be logical," Tuvok said. He looked into Janeway's startled gaze. "Anyone jumping within a Period would have the opportunity of causing paradoxes or altering the time line enough to destroy the entire culture."

Kjander's nodded. "It's what is taught as basic in the earliest classes in our schools. To us jumping outside of Period is so unthinkable as to almost not be imaginable. In fact, just suggesting it is a code violation. When your crew showed up it caused quite a stir and then when they tried to escape they got themselves into even more problems."

"How?" Janeway asked, almost afraid to hear the answer.

"They refused to go peacefully with a Time Control guard, so when they tried to escape back to the shuttle that brought them, they caused a Time Alarm."

"A Time Alarm."

"Time Control guards were forced to jump in time to a point right before they got to the ship. Causing a Time Alarm is also punishable by death."

"But you saw them alive?" Janeway asked.

Kjanders nodded. "When I left they were being escorted to Mean Time Control for Period Eight-eighty-nine. My guess is they will be taken from there to Mean Time Control Headquarters."

"When would that be?" Tuvok said.

"It's in Real Time in the First Period," Kjanders said.

The equation actually formed in Janeway's head. Her crew existed (889 × 500,000) + 300,000 years in the past.

"That's four hundred forty four *million* years," she said, almost to herself. She couldn't fathom that number. It was little more than a collection of zeros to her.

Tuvok let his templed hands fall to the table. He leaned toward Kjanders. "You seem quite calm for a man who accidentally wandered into a death sentence."

Kjanders looked up at Tuvok, startled.

"I assume you fall under the same regulations as our colleagues."

"Yes," Kjanders said, "but I'm not on Alcawell anymore. Control can't come up here."

Chakotay shot a knowing look at Tuvok. "Is that why you're here, Mr. Kjanders? To escape Control?"

"You brought me to the ship." Kjanders set down his fork. "I guess I have been remiss. A man really should say thank you to the people who have saved his life."

# CHAPTER
# 9

IF TORRES HADN'T KNOWN SHE HAD GONE OVER FOUR HUN-
dred million years into the past, she wouldn't have
been able to tell at first glance. The shuttle doors
opened into a shuttlebay remarkably similar to the
one so far away in the future.

"You folks don't really have an eye for interior
decoration, do you?" Neelix said to the guard who
brought them here.

The guard, as usual, ignored him.

Kim stepped out of the shuttle last. He glanced at
Torres, the panic making his dark eyes shine. Yet his
posture was straight, his bearing firm, as if he were
getting off a Starfleet shuttle near an Earth base.

The original guard led them down the ramp. The
other guards followed. Torres expected the air to taste
different or the temperature to be different, but the

underground caverns felt the same as before. The air had the taste of processing and the heat was turned up a bit too high.

A woman waited for them at the bottom of the ramp. She had purple hair piled in a cone that extended a meter and a half. Fortunately she had some distance between its tip and the ceiling. She wore a formfitting outfit of a shiny white material, and her purple shoes had pointy bases an eighth of a meter high. Jewelry sparkled in her hair.

"I'll take it from here," she said to the first guard. "You'll get a commendation for this. I've already put it in your record."

"Thanks, Cwaner," the guard said. He nodded to the other orange suits and they climbed back into the shuttle.

"You'd better get off the ramp," Cwaner said to Torres, Kim, and Neelix. "Unless you want to be slammed into the shuttle when they return to Eight-eighty-nine."

Torres led them off the ramp onto the hard floor. Cwaner looked perfectly balanced on her absurd shoes. "Welcome to Mean Time Control Headquarters. I am Cwaner, assistant to Rawlik. He will be examining your case."

"Will he be able to help us?" Kim asked.

"Help—?!" Cwaner smiled. "Yours is not to ask for help, but to be grateful for any kindnesses you receive."

"It's not in my nature to be grateful when I am about to be punished," Torres snapped.

Kim touched her arm. Neelix bobbed up and down at the woman as if he were trying to mollify her.

"Your headpiece," he said, speaking faster than usual, "reminds me of a spectacular headpiece I saw on an excursion seventeen years ago. It had precious jewels and a bit of gold woven through it, but it was white and not nearly as tall as yours. Do you dye it or can you find that color in nature?"

Cwaner raised a slender, eight-fingered hand to her hair. "It's an experiment," she said. "Do you like it? Rawlik said he preferred the blue."

"The purple brings out your eyes," Neelix said.

She smiled. "You should save your charm for Rawlik."

"Will it do us any good?" Torres asked.

Cwaner shrugged. "Not much can hurt you at this point."

She led them out of the shuttlebay into a long corridor that matched the one they had seen in Period 889. This corridor, though, was filled with flowering plants. Some had bright blue buds, others had black buds. Their odor was rich and pungent, reminding Torres of ointment her Klingon mother used to use to polish her breastplates.

The corridor led into an office complex filled with more flowering plants, desks, and people wearing tight variations of Cwaner's outfit. The shoes and hair were the most outrageous parts. It seemed that anything that made it impossible to walk was popular here.

Cwaner rapped on what looked like a stone wall three times with the knuckles of her right hand. The wall slid open, revealing an office almost half the size of the main room. One man sat behind a long black desk. He appeared to be in his late twenties. He had brown hair that touched his collar, a mustache, and, surprisingly, eyewear.

Computers, scattered papers, and stacks of 2-D photographs covered the surrounding tables. The chairs were a bright blue. Cwaner's hair clashed with the entire room. There were no plants in here, but there were many books, antique volumes that gave the room the smell of aging paper.

"Thanks, C-C," Rawlik said. His voice was soft.

She nodded in acknowledgment and backed out the door.

Torres waited until the door snicked shut before she launched herself at the desk. She planted both hands on it and leaned toward Rawlik.

"I am tired of people who can't help me, who quote regulations I have never heard of, and who accuse me of a crime when I am speaking according to my native custom."

Rawlik took off his eyewear, rubbed his eyes, and leaned back in his chair, a small grin playing on his face. "Welcome to Period One," he said.

"I am not welcome. I do not feel welcome. And I don't want your greetings," Torres said.

Kim touched her arm. "Relax," he said.

She shook him off. Time for going with this idiocy was through. "You look like someone important," she said. "I want to know if you can return us to our ship."

"That would be the Planet-Hopping ship in orbit

over the central station in Period Eight-eighty-nine?" Rawlik spoke with a slight drawl, choosing his words carefully.

"Our ship doesn't hop," Torres said. The anger she had been storing was seeping out the edges. Perhaps the thought of her Klingon mother had sent her over the edge. "It flies. Through space. From what I can tell we've hardly moved a kilometer in physical distance. I do not like traveling through time. Send us back to our ship and we will not trouble you again."

"I would like to," Rawlik said. He set his eyewear on the desk dangerously close to Torres's fists. The eyewear was tiny gold frames around clear lenses. "However, I can't. Please sit."

"Lieutenant," Kim said. "B'Elanna. Please. Let's do as he says."

Torres resisted the urge to snarl at the man. She sat at the edge of the nearest chair, ready to spring up at the slightest provocation. "All right," she said. "Tell me why you can't send us back."

"Frankly—Lieutenant?—you're lucky to be here at all. Control's Central Counsel will be reviewing your case because you are Planet-Hoppers. Let me point out that is a *good* thing. Usually citizens who break these laws are captured and punished without recourse."

"We had no idea we were breaking any laws when we arrived here, and we're still not certain which laws were broken," Torres said. "I'm sure we can come to some sort of understanding as long as you let us return to our ship."

"I'm afraid ignorance of the law is no excuse,"

Rawlik said. "And I can do nothing about that. Nor can I return you to your ship. I can, however, answer any questions you might have."

Questions? Torres had a thousand of them. She was about to ask one when Neelix grinned and opened his hands in his small conciliatory way.

"They keep mentioning punishment," Neelix said. "Now, I don't know about you, but as far as I'm concerned that word is a bit unpleasant. Perhaps if we knew what we were facing we might be able to temper our behavior to something appropriate for your culture."

Rawlik touched his computer screen. "It says here that you have at least one eight-hundred violation, two four-hundred violations—"

"They said they were going to waive those!" Neelix said.

"—and a possible six-hundred violation." Rawlik sighed. "The six-hundred violation is a misdemeanor. But the others are felonies, I'm afraid."

"Which means what?" Kim asked.

"The punishment is severe," Rawlik said. "Eight-hundred violations cover temporal tampering."

"We keep hearing this eight hundred stuff." Neelix said. "Just tell us what we did, please?"

"Your eight-hundred violation," Rawlik said, "was for traveling within a Period, which falls under a distinct class of regulations, which are divided into two subsets. Those tamperings committed with intent, and those committed without."

"We didn't intend to come here," Torres said.

"I know." Rawlik frowned. "You keep saying that.

But it makes no difference, really, except on your record. The punishment is the same."

"And that punishment is?" Neelix asked.

"Death."

The word hung in the processed air for a moment. Then Torres said, "Death?"

Rawlik nodded. "No exceptions. Eight-hundred violations are the most serious crimes possible."

"For most cultures murder is considered the most serious crime," Torres snapped.

"This is worse," Rawlik said. "Capital offenses within Real Time fall in the one-hundred violations. They have differing punishments."

"What can be worse than murder?" Neelix said.

"Temporal disturbances," Rawlik said. "In the wrong hands they can lead to genocide, the complete destruction of our culture, or the complete destruction of our world."

For the third time that day the breath left Torres's body. "We haven't done any of that, have we?"

"Not according to my records," Rawlik said. "But you did commit an eight-hundred violation. We can't change that."

Circles within circles within circles. Torres could barely tolerate Starfleet regulations. This bureaucratic doublespeak was making her dizzy.

"All right," she said. "We committed some kind of horrible crime that's somehow related to your time-travel culture. You had better explain culture, crime, and our involvement in language we 'Planet-Hoppers' can understand."

She crossed her arms and glared at him with a bravado she didn't quite feel.

Rawlik smiled at her and nodded. "I'll try."

"Please," she said. "And if you plan to kill me when you're through, this explanation better be damn good."

# CHAPTER
## 10

DRICKEL IGNORED HIS SMALL FLASHLIGHT IN FAVOR OF THE
lantern he had brought. Carefully, he took the lantern
out of his bag. He flicked the On switch and a flood of
light filled the pitch black caverns, making him feel
obscurely lonely. Normally he never felt lonely. Yet
here he was, in a time he hated, with only himself, his
bag, and unknown scavengers to count on.

It took him a moment to get his bearings. Each
movement in time included a bit of readjusting. As he
was getting older his body adjusted less quickly to the
changes in temperature and humidity. Not to mention
the other problems inherent in a shift. These old
Control caverns were so bone dry and dusty that any
fast movement he might make would send clouds of
choking dust into the air.

He turned slowly, studying the remains of the old

chamber. There were still some clay rings where the trees and flowers used to grow. The remains of a desk scattered across the floor and wires poked through the dust like gray snakes.

Even though he knew that this place had been abandoned because his people had found dimensional shifting more interesting than simple time travel, he still found the empty caverns spooky. Perhaps that had been the original inspiration for his behavior as a Watchman.

He swung the beam of the lantern toward the corridor. A wall on the right had caved in, causing a huge rock slide that sloped up into the ceiling. "Wonderful," he said.

His own voice echoed until it grew so faint he could no longer hear it. He wondered how far away the vibrations traveled. It was actually amazing that most of these old chambers were still open after so many years. They had been built solidly. He just hoped they were solid enough to hold together until he was out of them.

He put his bag over his shoulder and clamped the lantern to his side so as not to blind himself. As he started across the main room, clouds of dust billowed up with his every step. He kept moving, staying ahead of it. He found the old magnetic train tunnel right where he remembered it being from the maps.

The last time he'd jumped into this Control had been over twenty years Real Time ago, and then he had transported right to the surface from inside the smaller time chamber of the Back Room. He had caught scavengers who had jumped forward to the days after the Second Exodus. There had been six scavengers and it had been easy to scare them back to their Real Time without many problems. They had been a religious bunch and he'd played on those fears the way a professional musician played an Alcaharp.

Ten years earlier a small ship of Planet-Hoppers trying to salvage had set off another alarm in this Period. After a day of having equipment and metal appear and disappear around them as they tried to work, they had left orbit without so much as a souvenir. Planet-Hoppers, when faced with a huge ghost port like this one, were easily influenced by suggestion. In all his years, ghostlike antics had not failed him yet.

He studied the old magnetic railcar that was parked near the opening of the tunnel. The car was a small, oblong-shaped bullet made of once-shiny metal. Now, however, the car was buried in dust.

Carefully, he wiped the dust from the car's side, pulled on the handle, and winced at the *snap!* as the handle came off in his hand. He sighed, making dust particles float around him. It would have been nice to save himself the ten-kilometer walk and half-a-kilometer climb through the dark. Of course, he had just been dreaming, and a part of him knew it. Even in a dry climate like this, too many years had gone by since anything but a few shuttles had been serviced and maintained against the years.

Well, he was never one to shirk a good workout. He would get a sense of what kind of condition the tunnels were actually in. He dropped the handle in the dust, then started up the tunnel.

For the first half kilometer the tunnel went up at almost a forty-five-degree angle. He was sweating and covered with dust before he'd gone even a part of that distance. He slowed to a stop, letting the dust slowly settle around and behind him.

"This is stupid," he said, wiping dirt from his forehead. He was all for regulations—a Watchman should always use natural means of transport when available (Watchmen Regulations, Section 4,221, Article 96)—but not when those regulations asked him to be both grimy and exhausted.

He opened the bag and removed the control for his personal transporter. Some of the swirling dust finally caught in his throat and a coughing fit dislodged even more dust from the ceiling and walls. Dimly he was aware he was making matters worse.

Finally he held his breath, choking back any coughs that threatened, until the dust settled enough to be only a foglike substance swirling in the lamplight. Then he made himself breathe slowly, promising himself a deep satisfying cough attack when he reached the surface.

He flipped open the attached panel for the transporter on his belt. Then he opened the panel for the personal invisibility shields, located on the other side of his belt. Only Watchmen and high-security low-profile police were allowed invisibility shields (Watchmen Regulations, Section 66,719, Article 2), and for that he was grateful. It would make his job extremely difficult if the average Alcawellian even knew invisibility properties existed.

Still, invisibility wasn't perfect. For a fraction of a

second, he wouldn't be covered when he reached the surface. He couldn't transport and have his invisibility screen turned on at the same time. They hadn't solved that problem yet. Or at least hadn't given the solution to him yet. He would have to chance that the Planet-Hoppers wouldn't see him. They rarely had sensors that good, and even if they did, he'd be gone almost instantaneously. They'd never trace him.

He punched the transporter button and the next thing he felt was the cold wind blowing sand against his face like stinging hailstones.

"Wonderful climate," he said, turning away from the wind and keying in his invisibility shield. "I almost prefer the dust." He found his coat in his case and put it on, then snuggled a cap down over his head and put on a pair of goggles to protect his eyes from the flying sand.

With a quick glance around at all the broken-down old time shuttles, he started off at a steady pace toward the site where the Planet-Hoppers had touched down.

Janeway sat behind her desk in the ready room, her personal computer screen displaying the ship that had taken her away team from her. She had retired in here to study her options, review the situation, and to think about all that Kjanders had told them.

Like Chakotay, she didn't trust Kjanders. But he seemed to be telling the truth about the Alcawellian society. Tuvok and Chakotay had hit on the main problem, though. Kjanders seemed very unconcerned about his own possible death sentence.

She had confined him to quarters until she learned more.

She leaned back in her chair. Her ready room failed to soothe her. The view out the long windows included glimpses of Alcawell, and even though she couldn't see the hundreds of thousands of shuttles on the surface, she could picture them, lined up in their perfect rows. Sometimes she felt completely at sea in this part of the galaxy. Relying on Neelix only proved fifty percent effective. He got them help some of the time, and into trouble all the rest.

She only hoped he would be able to get them into trouble again because that would mean he was back on board.

She hadn't had time to check on Kes. The slight, pretty Ocampa had proven herself invaluable. Janeway knew that she would be having trouble, knowing that Neelix was a long way in the past.

Then Tuvok hailed her from the bridge. "Captain," he said. "I have a—"

His transmission stopped, but the link remained open. Curious. "What is it, Mr. Tuvok?" Janeway asked. She half rose from her seat, ready to go to the bridge.

"Forgive me, Captain," he said. "For a second my sensors registered a life-form on the planet's surface. Humanoid, about ten kilometers from the place the away team disappeared. Then it vanished without a trace."

"Is there a problem with the sensors, Mr. Tuvok?"

"I don't think so, Captain. It was almost as if the humanoid cloaked."

Janeway sighed. "Run a diagnostic and continue your sensor sweep. If that humanoid is cloaked and showed up once, the cloaking device is faulty. It'll show up again."

"I am on it, Captain."

"Good," Janeway said. She cut the link. Then she hailed Chakotay and asked him to join her in her ready room. Her options were limited, and she was facing several problems. She had to find her away team, as well as concentrate on keeping the ship in good order. She didn't want to think about how well *Voyager* would function if Torres never returned. Carey was a good engineer, but Torres was brilliant.

The door to the ready room hissed open and Chakotay entered. "You wish to see me, Captain?"

She nodded. "I've been considering the information our guest gave us. I'm reluctant to send another team down to the planet's surface, but I see no choice in the matter, do you?"

"A careful examination of the time shuttle would be, as Tuvok might put it, the logical thing to do," Chakotay said.

"Whom would you suggest?" Janeway asked. She'd been going over possibles. Realizing that none of them might come back made her evaluate everyone on the ship. None of them were dispensable. She was fortunate. Even though she was seventy-five years from home, she had been stranded with an excellent team.

She had thought of going herself, but knew that while her scientific knowledge was valuable, her abilities as captain were even more so.

"The choices are difficult," Chakotay said, "but I

too have been giving this some thought. Seska is an excellent engineer in her own right. Tuvok has knowledge that might help. I believe I would be a good choice for the team. I also feel it's my duty to inform you that Lieutenant Paris volunteered. He is anxious to find Kim and would like to help in any way he can."

Janeway permitted herself a small smile. Chakotay felt the same urge to be involved that she did. "I need you here. I'd like you to follow up on our guest, see if you can get more information from him. But the rest of your suggestions are good."

She stood. "Let's assemble the team."

Chakotay nodded. Together they left the ready room.

The bridge was quiet. Paris sat at conn, Tuvok was bent over his control panels at security, and Jarvin stood at ops. As Janeway walked toward the captain's chair, the turbolift opened. Kes left it. Her small face appeared composed, but she was twisting her hands together.

Janeway nodded at her, then turned to Tuvok.

"Mr. Tuvok, I am sending you, Lieutenant Paris, and Ensign Seska to the planet's surface. I want you to discover all you can about those ships without leaving us for the distant past. Is that understood?"

"Yes, Captain."

Paris stood. "Thank you, Captain. I've been worried about Kim."

"As have we all, Lieutenant. We're doing what we can. Assemble your supplies and meet in the transporter room. The sooner we move on this, the better off we'll be," Janeway said.

"Excuse me, Captain, but I would like to go as well." Kes's soft voice had a thread of strength running through it. She was difficult to deny.

Janeway turned to her. "I understand your desire to be involved," she said, "but I need mostly technical skill down there. When I find something you can help with, I will summon you immediately."

Kes looked at her hands as if they were betraying her; then she clasped them behind her back. Without that single repetitive movement, she appeared very calm. "May I stay on the bridge?"

"Of course," Janeway said. She faced Chakotay. "I want transporter locks at all times on the away team. If anything so much as moves down there, I want all of them back on board."

"Immediately, Captain," Chakotay said.

Tuvok contacted Seska and asked her to meet him in the transporter room. Then he motioned Paris to follow him, and headed for the turbolift. Paris was right beside him.

Janeway watched them go, hoping against hope that it wouldn't be the last time she would see them. But she had a bad feeling. A very bad one indeed.

# CHAPTER
## 11

His sensor beeped softly and Drickel ducked in behind the wreck of an old shuttle to get out of the incessant wind. He'd walked on the hard concrete for some distance and he was chilled to the bone. His legs ached from the climb through sand drifts and his cheeks felt as if the blowing sand had taken off the top three layers of skin. He doubted he would ever feel his nose again. Just once he wished the Planet-Hoppers would land in a warm climate. Just once.

He checked the sensor readings. Three Planet-Hoppers were working around an old shuttle a kilometer ahead. They hadn't entered it yet, but were staying outside in the wind for some reason. His sensors indicated they were running different types of scans on the craft. It took him a moment before he noticed the orange point of light that his sensors showed for the ship they were scanning.

His stomach twisted. That very ship was one of the few remaining ships kept in working condition for this time. How had they found it? He couldn't let them get on board. It was far too dangerous to use, and if they did happen to accidentally trigger a jump, they would find themselves in very serious problems back in Real Time.

He did a quick check of his invisibility device to make sure it was still functioning; then he took off at a quick jog through the tombstones of the old culture.

The ships towered over him, their sides and bottoms scarred from the wind and sand. Sometimes the unreality of his job struck him. Just a few hours before, he had ridden one of these shuttles. It had been in beautiful condition then and filled with passengers.

He ran silently, careful not to trip on anything. He left footprints in the sand, but the wind was so strong the prints were blown away as soon as he made them. His heart was pounding, not with effort, but with something close to fear. If he didn't reach those Planet-Hoppers in time, they would take a ride that would lead to almost certain death.

Finally he stopped in the shelter of a shuttle whose landing gear had given way. He tried to find a position where the swirling wind wouldn't blow sand in his nose. The three Planet-Hoppers were conferring near the foot of the ramp into the live ship. He could hear their voices, little sounds almost audible. The wind snatched away the words before he could make them out.

The Planet-Hoppers kept looking at the shuttle's door. He had arrived just in time.

The Planet-Hoppers were different from any people he had ever seen before. And different from each other. Two appeared to be male, one pale and the other dark. The dark male had pointed ears. The woman appeared to be a mixture of both. She had dark hair piled on top of her head, and light skin. Her nose had ridges, and she wore a large piece of jewelry on one ear. The jewelry jangled and snapped in the wind.

Their clothing was thin and not appropriate for the weather. As he watched, the woman ran her hands over her arms in an attempt to warm herself. Drickel grinned. Served them right for bringing him to this desolate place.

They weren't ready to go inside yet. He had a moment. He scanned the surrounding area among the broken shuttle and blown sand for anything that might scare them off. Twenty meters from him, half buried in sand, was a square metal plate blown off the outside of a ship. That would work for starters.

He grabbed a tiny antigravity disk from his belt, jogged to the plate, and placed the disk in the center of the metal. Holding the plate carefully with one hand so as to not obviously hide any of the metal with his invisibility, he floated it through the wind toward the three Planet-Hoppers. The plate bobbed and weaved slightly, like a young bureaucrat on new, impractical shoes. With the wind and blowing sand, the effect was eerie, just as he had hoped.

The tall pale man was the first to see the plate floating at them. He spun with what looked to be a weapon suddenly out and ready.

"Quick," Drickel murmured appreciatively.

The woman took a step back and also drew her weapon, while the pointed-ears man stood firm, staring intently at the plate. It wobbled as it approached them, its trajectory uncertain, its balance precarious. Drickel floated the plate within ten meters of the Planet-Hoppers and then let it fall. It landed with a clang on the pavement. The whistling of the wind and the faint rustling of the blowing sand soon took the sound away.

The pointed-eared one continued to stare at the plate while the other two, weapons drawn, scanned the entire area. Drickel chuckled to himself and moved back to the shelter of the nearby ship, being careful to not step in any sand drifts.

As he watched the three talked loudly, but not loud enough for him to hear through the wind. Finally the pointed-eared one walked slowly over and prodded the edge of the heavy plate with his foot. When it didn't move that way, he crouched and tried to lift the edge. He managed to get it a few centimeters off the ground. Then he let it fall. He took out an instrument that looked like some sort of scanning device. First he used the instrument to scan the plate. Then he swept the scanner over the entire area.

Drickel was glad he had double-checked his invisibility device.

Pointed Ears shook his head, and said something over his shoulder to the others. They looked as skeptical as he did.

"He's going to be a tough sell," Drickel said under his breath. He would have to try something more impressive. No woo-woo noises and floating plates for these Planet-Hoppers. He needed something that would defy their understanding of reality.

He glanced at the ship that rose over his head. The three landing legs had given away and time had eroded most of the base. The ramp had been smashed underneath when it fell. Part of the door was visible and open and sand had filled the interior. A large drift of sand had formed on one side.

The entire ship looked as if it would crumble in the next big wind gust. Only the extremely dry climate had kept it in one piece this long. It would be perfect for a great effect.

Drickel opened up his bag and pulled out the antigravity pads. It would take three to lift this old hulk, but the effort would be worth it.

He worked his way around the wreck, placing the antigravity pads equal distances apart and being careful again to not leave deep prints in any sand. Then he moved over to the downwind side of another wrecked shuttle and pulled the remote control out of his bag.

The three Planet-Hoppers still stood near the metal plate talking and running occasional scans. They were talking animatedly as they did so. The pale man was gesturing as he spoke. The woman still had her arms clasped around herself, her teeth obviously chattering.

She glanced around every few moments. If they had a weak link, she was it, he would wager.

Pointed Ears remained focused on the plate. He scanned it again, pointed at something on the readout, and frowned. He seemed unconcerned by the cold or the wind. The pale man's face had turned red in the weather. The woman was speaking now with such force that her head bobbed with each word.

He aimed the remote at the old wreck. "Let's see how they like this."

Metal screeched against metal, jarring Drickel's teeth, and sending shivers down his back. Then the old shuttle lurched from the sand and pavement that had held it for a thousand years. It rose five meters.

"Nice," Drickel said to himself at the effect.

Crushed landing gear and the old ramp dangled like broken limbs under the wreck. The wind gave it a slightly shifting look as the antigravity units kept it level.

The legs banged and smashed around in the wind until one finally tore loose and fell back to the pavement.

The Planet-Hoppers had all turned at the first noise and then taken several steps back from the rising wreck. The pale man watched, then scurried around slightly to one side, apparently to get a different view. The woman just stood, mouth open, hands clutching her elbows. She suddenly looked less cold and more frightened. Drickel would have counted the moment a success if not for Pointed Ears. He had out his sensory device and had it aimed at the floating wreck.

"Don't spook easy, do you?" Drickel said. "How

about this?" He slowly moved the ship in the direction of the three. Its remaining landing gear dragged along against the pavement, scraping and grinding as it moved. The wind howled around them. This sound was even more unsettling than the first one.

All three Planet-Hoppers took another step back in unison. The woman put her hands over her ears, and the pale one was wincing at the noise. Old Pointed Ears slapped his chest and said something Drickel couldn't hear over the horrible noise. A moment later all three sparkled and then vanished.

"Transporter beams," Drickel said. "Impressive."

He immediately raised the ship a bit higher so that the scraping, grinding, and howling would end. Then he spent the next ten minutes staying out of the wind while moving the wrecked shuttle around in circles, even once bumping it against another wreck. He figured the Planet-Hoppers were probably scanning from orbit. He didn't want them to tie their presence to the strange event.

Finally he lowered the wrecked shuttle back to its place in the rows of wrecks. The ship disintegrated when it landed—the legs crumpled beneath it, the ramp shattered, and sand spilled out of the door.

Amazing how time controlled everything.

It took more effort than he wanted to expend to retrieve his antigravity pads, but he did it anyway. No point in leaving anything around for the Planet-Hoppers to find if they were brave enough to return.

Then he moved away from the live shuttle down one row until he found an old wreck still standing on its landing gear with its ramp still fully extended. It wasn't in the best of shape, but it would do.

He quickly walked inside. Without the wind, the air seemed much warmer. He wiped the sand off his face and hoped he was done with this mission. He would wait the designated day after they left orbit and then return to his warm jungle home.

Janeway stopped in surprise as she entered the briefing room. Paris, Tuvok, and Seska were seated at the table. All three had their hands wrapped around steaming mugs. They still wore their jackets and they all had windburn on their cheeks. Paris's nose was still red. Seska's Bajoran earring was tangled around her ear.

Carey entered just behind Janeway, as did Chakotay and Kes. They took their usual places at the table, with Janeway at the head.

"All right, people," she said. "I want impressions as well as information. Tuvok."

Tuvok took a quick sip of his Vulcan spice tea—the only sign that he was at all uncomfortable—and said, "We observed two unexplained movements of equipment that should not, as far as I could ascertain, have moved. I do not yet know what caused the movements, although I do believe that the movements are not directly related to the shuttle that the first away team disappeared in."

"Equipment?" Paris kept one hand wrapped around his mug, and rested his other elbow on the back of his chair. "That's an understatement. One piece of equipment was a wreck twice the size of a shuttlecraft and older than God. The thing was moving through the air, sand seeping out of the door and the holes in its frame, and the wind was howling through it. Forgive me for being emotional about this, but I found it damn creepy."

"So did I," Seska said.

"Considering the weight and age of the craft, and the fact that it had no obvious means of propulsion," Tuvok said, "it was an impressive show."

*"Impressive* was not the word that came to my mind," Paris said.

Seska nodded. She fiddled with her earring, her eyes wide.

Janeway glanced at Paris. He was excitable—that was part of his charm—but he rarely exaggerated events. If anything, he minimized. The sight of that ruined ship moving through the air must have been impressive indeed.

"Captain," Tuvok said, ignoring Paris, "the ruined ship continued hovering six point three minutes after we beamed back to *Voyager.*"

"Maybe Neelix was right," Kes said. "Maybe the place is haunted."

Everyone in the room looked at Kes. Tuvok raised an eyebrow and, to Janeway's surprise, Paris did not grin. An uneasy silence filled the room.

Finally, Seska said, "Bajorans are raised to believe there are many things we cannot see. We should never discount the spiritual aspect of any journey."

"Are you saying there are ghosts on the planet?" Janeway asked.

Seska took a deep breath. "With one look at that ship, you knew it was too dilapidated to work. Yet it came right at us. I don't know if I think that is the work of a ghost, but I do know that the entire experience was unnerving."

"Perhaps intentionally," Tuvok said. "The metal plate clearly moved toward us and fell at our feet as almost a warning."

Paris nodded. "That's why it felt so creepy," he said. "It was almost as if something on the surface knew we were there and didn't want us around."

"That and the wind," Seska said. "The noise alone was enough to unsettle anyone."

"If the ruined ship were moved to scare us, or to make the place seem 'haunted,' it would be logical to continue the movement after the interlopers left. That way the movement would seem unrelated to our presence." Tuvok took another sip of his spice tea. His cheeks were still greenish-brown from the wind, but his hands looked warmer.

"If those time shuttles still function," Janeway said, "I understand the need to keep trespassers off the planet. It would be disastrous to have strangers appear three hundred thousand years in the past. But that doesn't solve our problem. We still don't know how to find our away team."

Paris looked up. "Do you think this Kjanders might know something about this?"

"I don't think so," Chakotay said. "I just spent the last half hour with him and he seems much more interested in our ship than the planet below. He also seemed surprised and shaken by the condition of the shuttle field below. But I will ask him."

"Please," Janeway said. She glanced around again. "Any more suggestions?"

"Captain," Chakotay said. "One more thing about Kjanders. I believe that confining him to quarters does us no good. I believe he's up to something. If we know what it is, we might be able to get more answers out of him."

"Very well, Chakotay," Janeway said, "we'll let him out of quarters after you brief the crew. We'll have everyone keep an eye on him."

Chakotay leaned back, apparently satisfied.

"I have been thinking, Captain, about the planet below," Tuvok said. "If we return to the planet's surface, we should find whoever or whatever is moving the equipment around. We might be able to get information about our away team."

"Good suggestion, Tuvok," Janeway said.

"Also," Tuvok said, "if it turns out to be one of the time travelers, he might have a way to return to the past without having to trust the old shuttle that kidnapped our crew."

"So we're going ghost hunting," Paris said. He shook his head and downed the last of his hot drink. "Wonderful."

Janeway looked at him. "I take it you are volunteering again?"

Paris nodded. "Can't let a Vulcan have all the fun. He wouldn't appreciate it."

Tuvok glanced at him without a smile.

"See what I mean?" Paris said.

# CHAPTER

# 12

KJANDERS STEPPED OUT OF THE QUARTERS THAT CAPTAIN Janeway had so nicely provided for him, and the door hissed closed behind him. He had never before been in such an orderly place. Even the colors on *Voyager* were tame. No bright oranges, no deep purples. A lot of grays, soft blues, and an occasional black line for definition.

The request that Kjanders had just received from Chakotay sounded a lot more like an order than an entreaty. This ship, while seeming more benign, was much more structured than Alcawell had ever been. Kjanders doubted he could duck into the background here and expect to remain forgotten.

His quarters were a case in point. In the short time they had confined him there, he had had a visitor, several communications, and an inquiry after his health from the guard outside. The inquiry had startled him the most—he had been investigating an out-of-order machine on the wall which, the computer told him, used to make food. He had been clanging around inside the machine when the guard had called in to him.

The guard was gone now. And even though people nodded to him as they passed in the corridor, they seemed less interested in him than they had been before. Good. He hoped that trend would continue. He didn't want to call much more attention to himself. Sometimes he thought Chakotay saw too much as it was.

Kjanders glanced at the diagram of the ship on the wall across from his quarters. The ever-present computer, the diagrams, the passing uniformed crew made him feel as if he had stumbled into a branch of Control. A branch that knew how to eat well and wear comfortable clothing, but a branch all the same.

Once he located the turbolift, he strode down the hall at the same confident pace as the rest of *Voyager*'s crew. Perhaps if they gave him a uniform. Yes. That might work. He would have to modify his hairstyle, but that wouldn't bother him. The more he looked like them, the more they might accept him.

He stepped onto the turbolift and asked it to stop on the level with the officers' mess. It made a slight hum as it rose. He found it odd that these Starfleet people did not use transporters to move around their ship. The ship was large enough that if it existed on Alcawell, it would have a set of internal transporters on each level. Starfleet seemed to put a higher premium on foot travel than Alcawellians did.

When he entered the officers' mess, he stopped as he had the first time and stared out the windows into the darkness of space. Alcawell was partially visible, its surface empty and cold. The memory of his arrival made him shudder.

"Well," Chakotay said. "You arrived." He was standing near one of the tables. He had a plate covered with yellow bread in his hand. At the table were two steaming mugs.

"Yes," Kjanders said. "It wasn't as difficult as I thought it would be."

"Good." Chakotay put the bread down, and sat. "I asked for corn bread yesterday. They made it for me today, once they were convinced they had the ingredients. Would you like some?"

Kjanders sat beside him and took a bit of bread. It had a surprisingly sweet taste.

Chakotay smiled. "A bit of home," he said. "As is the coffee. Strong and black."

Kjanders picked up his mug.

"Be careful," Chakotay said. "It's bitter."

Anything that smelled that rich couldn't be bitter. Kjanders took a sip and nearly spit it out. He made himself swallow. "You drink this?" he said.

"Most people put sugar and cream in it." He pulled two other dishes closer. "I like mine strong and nasty."

The words had an ominous ring. Kjanders ignored them. He shoved sugar into his mug, sipped, and decided to add the cream as well. When the liquid was only slightly darker than the milk, he finally decided he liked the taste.

"I take it you didn't invite me for a friendly meal," Kjanders said.

"No." Chakotay took a bite of corn bread, then sipped his coffee. "I want you to know that I'm the one who got the guard called off your door and got you the freedom to walk through the ship."

Kjanders smiled. "This time I'll remember to say thanks."

"Good," Chakotay said as if the thanks didn't matter at all. "I want you to know, though, that I understand you. I realize you're running from something. I don't want that something to interfere with anything on this ship."

Kjanders felt hot. He made himself take another sip of his own coffee. How much had Chakotay figured out? Kjanders hadn't done anything to give away his intention of taking over this ship.

"So I would suggest you cooperate with me in getting our team back."

"This sounds like a repeat of the conversation we had a Real Time hour ago, Commander," Kjanders said.

"It isn't." Chakotay leaned toward him. Kjanders suddenly realized that Chakotay was a large man who wore his power very well. "We've just discovered movement on the planet. Ships lifting off that shouldn't be able to run, equipment flying on its own, possibly to scare our people who were investigating below. I want to know if someone came with you or if someone came after you to this time."

The coffee's bitterness came through all the sweeteners. Kjanders stomach turned. "I hope not," he said, allowing his nausea to show. "If they did, they'll take me back and then I'm a dead man."

"Is it customary to send someone after a time violator?" Chakotay asked.

Kjanders shrugged. "That would fall under the eight-hundred violations, and most of those are classified. We all know the laws and the punishments, but not how the enforcement is carried out. If we knew any more than that, time would be threatened."

Chakotay turned his head. He took another bit of his piece of corn bread, chewed, and swallowed. "You still haven't told me if you arrived alone."

"You had me on your scanners. You know I did." Kjanders's voice rose just a bit. His Control analogy wasn't far off.

"And you have no idea what could cause the problems down there?"

Kjanders shook his head. He really didn't want to think about the emptiness below. "For all I know," he said, "it could have been the wind."

Torres paced back and forth across their cell. The fact that they were in something that resembled crew quarters on the ship didn't make this any less a prison. Kim sat on an overstuffed chair, and Neelix reclined on a chaise longue, his hands clasped behind his head. Torres walked past the flowering plants (she had already picked the blooms off and tossed them into a disposal—the smell was bringing back too many memories of growing up) and into the barren kitchen.

Not a weapon in sight.

Not that she expected one. It wouldn't have mattered if they had one. Rawlik had let them keep their phasers. The "back-timing" trick that the guards had took care of any problem. Torres could stun someone only to have her phaser confiscated a few moments earlier.

Her head ached from all the double-thought this time travel culture required. Rawlik had explained everything carefully, even answering Neelix's questions—

*(But what good is traveling 500,000 years if you're stuck at the same desk day after day? Wouldn't you want adventure?)*

—all the time maintaining eye contact with Torres. She couldn't tell if he found her attractive or annoying. Probably neither. Not that it mattered anyway. He was part of the Control that planned to kill her.

She had had her run-ins with bureaucracies before. It took a pretty special person to cut all the red tape.

Neelix believed Rawlik was that person. Torres wasn't sure.

She paced to the door, opened it, and peered down the hall. The same orange-suited guard stood outside. He smiled at her. These people were awfully friendly for jailers. She preferred a bit more rudeness from people who were going to commit something as personal as murder.

She slammed the door shut.

"Eventually," Neelix said without opening his eyes, "the door will shatter and they'll slap another violation on us. What do you think the penalty is for door-shattering?"

"Death," Kim said. His tone was dry. "After all, it does affect travel."

Torres frowned. She remembered Kim's dark sense of humor from when she had been trapped with him in the Ocampa Hospital. No wonder he was able to keep himself superficially calm during all this turmoil. He had a running commentary of dry, witty remarks to keep himself distracted.

"I don't find that funny," Torres said. "We should be working on a way out of here."

"They've made it easy," Kim said. "We have our phasers and the door isn't locked. The guard isn't strong enough to fight the three of us."

"There's just this little matter of an underground cavern and four hundred and forty four million years," Neelix said. He opened his eyes. When he was serious, he looked a bit like a wet puppy. "I hope Kes is all right."

"I'm sure she's fine," Torres said. "She's on *Voyager*. And how can you be so relaxed? It was your naps that got us in trouble in the first place."

"Talaxians have more need of sleep than humans do." He paused, looked a bit chagrined. "Or Klingons. Or whatever you're calling yourself today."

"I think my Klingon side is beginning to become dominant." Torres said each word slowly and with emphasis. "And for once I don't believe I'll fight it."

At that statement Kim stood up and blocked her

path. "Lieutenant, I think you're right. I think we should figure out how to get out of here."

"After I kill Neelix," she said, but did not push past Kim.

"Don't worry," Neelix said. "The Mean people will soon take care of that for you." He sat up, yawned, and then stretched. He stood, walked to the kitchen, and banged around the cupboards for a moment.

"They named themselves well," he mumbled. "Only Mean people would give us such a wonderful kitchen and forget the food. I was hoping to whip up some breakfast, since my stomach tells me it is that time of the day."

Torres sat on the nearest chair so hard that it groaned beneath her weight. Maybe her Klingon side was dominating, because she was hungry. Her stomach was growling. She had just ignored it with everything else going on.

Kim remained in the middle of the room, as if he expected Torres to spring across any moment and attack Neelix. She wouldn't. She knew better. It was just that sometimes the little man got on her nerves.

Seriously on her nerves.

Faint laughter floated through the door. Kim turned toward it. Torres sat up. Neelix came out of the kitchen holding a small shiny pan. A moment later Rawlik walked in, smiling.

"Ah," Neelix said to Kim, "a smile. It's a friendly smile too. I hope this means we're about to be rescued."

"Well," Rawlik said, "we're a step closer. I got the council to postpone their decision until tomorrow."

"Postpone?" Kim asked. "What does that mean?"

"It means we're not going to die tonight," Torres said.

Rawlik glanced at her, his expression soft and sympathetic. "Each delay is promising."

"I heard that when I was applying for Starfleet Academy," Torres said.

"And you got in," Kim said.

Rawlik sat beside Torres. The man was sensitive. He didn't sit too close, but he wasn't too far away either. "I promise you," he said as if he were speaking to her only, "that I will be working through the night to find anything I can find to save you. We are not a barbaric society. We just have some very strict laws about breaking the time-travel restrictions."

"Very strict," Neelix said. *"Veeeeery* strict. So strict, in fact, that I would hate to see your definition of rigid."

Rawlik shot Neelix an uncertain glance. Kim sat down across from Rawlik. "I'm sorry," Kim said. "We do appreciate all that you're doing for us. The day has been a bit stressful and being hungry isn't helping."

Rawlik looked shocked for a moment. "I never thought," he said. "I will have dinner brought here to you."

*A bit stressful?* Torres mouthed behind Rawlik's back.

Kim ignored her. "Thanks," he said. "We'd appreciate it."

Yes. They all appreciated one last meal. "Tell me,"

Torres said, "What are you planning to do in our defense tomorrow?"

Rawlik turned to her. He did like her. She could see it in his eyes. Not that she had given him any encouragement. Not that their friendship had any real future.

"I'm afraid," he said, "there is no defense for what you've done. It is a matter of record. I honestly believe the only hope is to plead your ignorance of our culture and then plead for mercy."

"Has that ever worked?" Neelix asked from across the room.

"No," Rawlik said softly. "It never has."

# CHAPTER

# 13

As the transporter beam released him, Paris glanced around at the windblown surface of the planet. The ghost shuttle was back in place and the wind had already erased most of the marks in the sand from the dragging ramp. The metal plate that had first floated at them was already covered by sand, with the wind piling more around it by the minute.

Paris pulled out his tricorder while beside him Tuvok did the same. The captain had decided that this time only the two of them would beam down. They weren't so much working on the shuttle as looking for whoever or whatever was moving things around.

Paris scanned the area to his right, while Tuvok scanned the area to the left. Sand, sand, and more sand. Beneath bits of metal and pavement. "Nothing," Paris said.

Tuvok nodded and moved purposefully across the opening between the ships toward the ghost ship. Paris followed, pulling the collar on his coat up as high as it would go to protect his face from the stinging bite of the blowing sand. This was the driest planet Paris had ever been on. He could feel his nose clog up and his eyes fight to keep enough moisture. And they were on the winter side of the planet. He didn't want to imagine what the summer would be like—sand and concrete surrounded by thousands of huge hunks of metal. The heat would be as intense as the cold.

Tuvok moved straight toward the ghost ship, not seeming even to notice the wind.

Tuvok never seemed to notice anything. Sometimes Paris thought Vulcans had turned off parts of their bodies except their brains. If Paris ever did that he would have nothing left to live for. A bit of excitement, a beautiful woman, and a ship to pilot were all he asked for out of life. He didn't care if he had the same woman or the same ship from day to day, but he did care if he missed out on his excitement.

He was hoping, just hoping, that the ghost would reappear and attempt to scare them again. The last time had been a touch frightening. This time would be exhilarating.

And if the ghost could lead them to Kim and the others, Paris would be damn pleased.

Damn pleased.

Tuvok stopped near the ghost shuttle and used his tricorder to scan the shuttle at close range. Sometimes Tuvok's tricorder seemed to be an extension of his brain. Together they learned things that Paris could just guess at. Still, Tuvok would need Paris when it came time to rush the ghost. Sometimes the logical, considered reaction was not the best reaction.

Apparently Tuvok's tricorder didn't pick anything up, because he moved another few steps. Paris turned his back to the wind, keeping his gaze on Tuvok at all times. Sure, *Voyager* could beam them up if they got separated, but in this cold and wind, the wrong few minutes alone could be deadly.

Paris scanned the surrounding shuttles for any movement besides wind. Nothing. This place was as dead as any place he'd ever seen. What had Kjanders said? That this place was once alive and flowing with people? Paris found that almost hard to believe.

Tuvok nodded to himself and moved around the shuttle, stopping every few meters to take another scan. Paris followed closely behind, guarding Tuvok's back.

On the other side of the wreck the landing gear had collapsed under the weight, and parts of the ramp provided a wedge, leaving the shuttle canted at an odd angle. That angle was just enough to protect them from the wind, and Tuvok motioned they should go under there.

Without the sand blowing at them, the pocket of calm felt almost livable. Paris wiped his face and looked at Tuvok. Sand crusted Tuvok's upswept eyebrows, giving him a look of great age.

They could talk here without shouting.

"Anything?" Paris asked.

Tuvok nodded and pointed upward. "See that faint dent in the plate there?"

Paris studied the plate until he saw what Tuvok was pointing toward. A dent in a very old piece of metal that no one would notice. "Yeah."

Tuvok checked his tricorder again. "A small anti-gravity device was attached there not too long ago. Two other similar devices were spaced around this ship."

Paris scanned the area, but couldn't find the anomaly that led Tuvok to his conclusion. That didn't surprise him. Paris was a bit casual on some of his science—when it didn't apply to piloting. He was willing to trust Tuvok. "Any idea who did this?"

"Unknown," Tuvok said. "But it seems that our 'ghost,' as you have all been calling him, uses technology to achieve his effects."

"You were worried?" Paris said.

Tuvok gave him a measured gaze. "Of course not."

"So now that we know a living agent brought about these spectral events, how come it hasn't come for us again?" Paris asked.

"Because," Tuvok said, "we have not approached the item it is protecting."

Paris stared at Tuvok for a moment before he said, "The working time shuttle."

Tuvok nodded. "Exactly."

"Logical," Paris said.

"Of course," Tuvok said without so much as even a smile. He led the way back across the open, wind-blown area between the shuttles. The first blast of wind-driven sand felt like tiny pieces of broken glass hitting his skin. Paris brought his collar up even higher, wishing he had thought to wear some kind of extreme-weather gear.

They stopped at the bottom of the ramp of the shuttle that had taken the first away team and brought back Kjanders. They used their tricorders to scan for any movement or signs of anything. Paris got nothing. Not a movement, not a sign of life. Nothing.

Finally Tuvok moved about halfway up the ramp and stopped, waiting, holding up his tricorder, getting readings of the surrounding area.

Paris stopped a meter below him and did the same. Nothing moved. Nothing floated at them.

"I'm going to widen my scan," Paris said, shouting in the wind. "Our ghost might be coming from a distance."

Tuvok nodded. "I will study the ship while you stand guard." Tuvok turned and moved another few steps up the ramp, his gaze intent on the tricorder in his hand.

Paris walked down the ramp, wincing at the strength of the wind. Alcawellians didn't want to leave this place? They preferred traveling through time to traveling in space? Obviously they didn't know that the vast universe had other things to offer besides cold, driving winds.

Using the ship as the center of a circle, he estimated the distance between the other ships and methodically opened up the scan by that distance. He carefully scanned the full circle around the ship, paying close attention to the area blocked from their sight on the other side of the shuttle. He knew that on board

*Voyager,* Lieutenant Carey was also continuously scanning the area, but at the moment Paris wished it were Kim up there. Paris trusted Carey, but he'd have just felt better if it were Kim.

It wasn't until he widened his field of scan a second time to the distance of about five of the old wrecks away that he caught movement to the north.

He tapped his comm badge, opening the link to Carey in Engineering. "Lieutenant, focus down on an area about half a kilometer to our north."

There was a moment of silence, then Carey came back on. "I have some small movement inside a shuttle five wrecks down from you. Nothing alive. Just slight movement of what looks to be a piece of ceiling panel on one of the old ships. Might be normal settling and collapse. I'm getting lots of that kind of reading throughout the field with the wind kicking up the way it is this time of the day."

"Thank you. Paris out." That reading from Carey confirmed the readings Paris had. But there was something odd about this one and he just couldn't dismiss it. He wasn't sure why. That wouldn't play well with a Vulcan. He sighed, shielded his eyes, and faced the ramp, motioning Tuvok to join him.

Paris told Tuvok what he had seen and that Carey had confirmed it. Then he said, "I know the wind is blowing like a son of a gun out here, and I know these ships are going to settle. I just can't believe one would settle this close to us."

Tuvok glanced at him, then back at his own tricorder. Paris could see he was doing another quick scan of the area. When it came up negative, he looked back up at Paris.

Paris shrugged. "Call it a hunch. I never abandon a hunch."

Tuvok nodded. "We are getting nowhere here. Examining another site would be logical."

Paris grinned. "Great. I didn't think convincing you would be this easy."

"I have been around humans a long time," Tuvok said. "And, over the years, I have learned that hunches are often based on things seen but improperly processed. You probably read something you failed to understand and yet you had enough sense to know it was important."

"Ouch," Paris said. "I think I've just been insulted."

"Logic is never personal," Tuvok said and started to walk toward the north.

"Yes," Paris said, "but the dissemination of it often is." He pulled up his collar again to keep the sand out of his shirt and off his neck and followed Tuvok to the mystery ship.

Drickel had been dozing for the last hour, waiting for the Planet-Hoppers to return as he knew they would. The ship he had found still open and sitting on its landing gear was deteriorated almost beyond belief. But inside, the old padding ripped off two chairs offered a decent couch for his nap. Besides, in the ship he was out of the wind. He thought of setting up a heating device, but decided against it. The Planet-

Hoppers above might be able to sense that sort of thing. Ghosts didn't need heat. At least the type of ghost he was trying to pretend to be.

The alarm in his earpiece woke him when the Planet-Hoppers' transporter beam dropped them near the live ship. He stretched and moved, stiffer than he wanted to be thanks to the cold.

The Planet-Hoppers' persistence annoyed him. If they had been scared away the first time he would have been able to return to home and warmth shortly. But he had had a bad feeling when he saw Pointed Ears. The ghost trick had worked on every other scavenger, but this one seemed intrigued by the events rather than frightened. And intrigued was the exact opposite reaction from the one Drickel wanted.

Drickel double-checked to make sure his shield was still in place so the Planet-Hoppers wouldn't see or sense him. It was. He stood, clicked on his small light, and stretched.

"Time to go play ghost again," he said to himself, and his voice sounded hollow in the almost dark interior of the ship. He did a few quick stretching exercises to loosen his muscles, and as he did, he pondered the problem of Pointed Ears. Maybe only harmless ghosts intrigued the Planet-Hopper. Drickel didn't want to hurt anyone, but threats were something he would find acceptable. It would take a lot of control—he certainly wouldn't be able to use a ship again—but he could do it. If old Pointed Ears thought his life in danger, he might never set foot on Alcawell again.

Drickel finished his exercises, then stepped toward the door to pick up his bag and be on his way.

At that moment the vibrations of his movement in the old ship, possibly combined with the wind, loosened a metal ceiling panel. It gave way and dropped.

He caught enough of a glimpse of it coming, and the sound of it letting loose also warned him just in enough time to get his hand above his head.

The heavy panel hit his arm, smashing him to the floor and coming to rest with half of it on his shoulder and the rest over his lower body.

His head banged hard against the floor and his ears rang.

He tried to cover his head with his good arm, thinking that more things from the ceiling would come crashing down.

But nothing did.

He waited, staying perfectly still, holding his breath. Nothing more.

And after a moment it was clear that nothing was going to come down immediately.

Then the pain started, a jabbing shot that ran from his arm to his hand and back into his chest. He closed his eyes and thought, not allowing himself to panic.

His movements in the shuttle must have released the already loose ceiling panel. A mistake on his part. He should have checked the shuttle more thoroughly before using it as a base. When he got back he would ask Control not to send him to any more cold destinations. His desire to be warm had made him careless.

And might have gotten him seriously injured.

He took a slow breath, checking to see if any ribs were broken. It didn't seem so, but his mouth and throat were totally caked with the dust.

He slowly opened his eyes to get his bearings.

His lamp was still working near his bag, doing its best to light up the billowing clouds of dust. He was on his side and his legs, hips, and shoulders were pinned under the weight of the heavy metal panel. His arm ached and he could tell he was going to have one hell of a headache.

He just hoped the panel falling on him hadn't broken his shielding. The Planet-Hoppers would spot him for sure.

Taking two deep breaths choked with dust, he tried to raise the metal plate off his shoulders. Pain shot through his right arm and he quit pushing. The plate had moved, but it was going to be a slow and very painful process to get it off himself. If he didn't do it right, he would end up with more than just a hurt arm. This plate was so heavy it would crush a hand or a foot, and then what would he do?

If he could move his arm down to his belt he might be able to reach his transporter and beam himself out. But he would also have to shut off his shield to do that, thus showing himself to the Planet-Hoppers. That would be his last option. He wanted to try to remove the plate himself first.

He took another deep breath and tried to lift the edge of the plate with his shoulder. It did move, but not enough to make much difference. It was too bad his bag was so far away, with its antigravity disks. He could have floated this off in an instant. He looked around for something he could use to pull his bag toward him, but saw nothing. It was two meters away and totally out of reach.

His only physical choice was to crawl out carefully and very slowly. He just hoped the Planet-Hoppers were staying away from that working shuttle. Because this was going to take some time.

# CHAPTER
## 14

JANEWAY NORMALLY GOT A LOT OF IDEAS IN HER READY room, but the ideas that were coming to her over Alcawell did not please her at all. She stood in front of the long windows, staring down at the planet, a cup of traditional coffee cooling on her desk. Chakotay had brought it to her. He was sitting in a chair behind her, waiting, with a patience she could never mimic, for her to explain why she had brought him here.

Finally she sighed. Whether she liked the idea or not didn't matter. What mattered was if it would get results.

"Chakotay," she said as she turned to face him. "I think we have to send another away team into the past."

He crossed his arms, but did not look startled. "I trust you've examined the risks," he said.

She nodded. She was relieved that he didn't try to review all the arguments against the trip, as her first officer on her last commission did. "I've decided that we've put too much stock in Kjanders. None of us trust him. If he's speaking the truth we will lose both teams. But if he's not, we'll get both teams back."

"You've never shirked risk before," Chakotay said. "After all, you tried to capture *me.*"

Janeway smiled, at Chakotay's joke and at his calm acceptance of her idea. She walked down the steps toward his chair.

"It seems to me," Janeway said, "that instead of studying the working ship that we found, we should be tearing into the other inoperative ships around it to figure out how they used to work. We know their time travel uses chroniton particles in some fashion or another. If we can at least discover how the tracking works on those other shuttles, we might be able to use their technology to track an away team through time."

Chakotay nodded, thinking. "That just might work, but what—"

"Captain," Lieutenant Carey's voice broke in. Both Chakotay and Janeway paused. "I think I found something you'll want to see."

Janeway and Chakotay stood in unison and headed for the door. It slid open quickly and they both hurried to the bridge.

Carey stood at the security console. "I was running standard scans for movement in the area around the away team," he said as soon as he saw Chakotay and Janeway, "when it occurred to me that there may be movement in the old tunnels belowground. So I expanded my scans to search below the surface."

Janeway and Chakotay crowded in beside Carey. He brought up a screen that showed a tunnel, fairly large and running in two directions. "This tunnel is a quarter of a kilometer below the surface," Carey said, "and fairly close to the area below Tuvok and Paris. I followed it and expanded my search to cover the entire base. Here's what I found."

He tapped the console, changing the screen picture. First he showed the huge base; then he overlaid a very clear pattern of black lines and spots over it. He placed a large spot in the middle of the screen. The picture looked like a spider with a huge number of legs. The body of the spider was a large cavern. Janeway glanced at the readout. The main cavern was a kilometer below the surface.

"I found most of this in the initial searches," Chakotay said.

"I know, sir," Carey said. "These caverns, like everything else down there, are all long abandoned. Almost all, that is."

Janeway glanced at Carey. He was bouncing on his toes, ever so lightly, but enough to make himself bob. This discovery had him excited for the first time since the original away team disappeared. He had found something important.

"On a hunch," he said, "I scanned the underground chamber for the chroniton particles similar to the ones the shuttle emits." He paused for a moment, then pulled up a new overlay. "I found this."

Janeway leaned forward so she could see the screen better. Near one side of the main underground chamber, in a much smaller room, was a strong source of chroniton particles, continuous and flowing.

"After I called for you," he said, "I scanned the entire base for traces of those particles."

Five more green dots appeared on the map. Janeway's heart started to pound hard. Finally, something that they might be able to use. She wasn't sure how yet, but she knew they had made a breakthrough.

"Captain," Carey said, "the shuttle that took the first away team is still omitting a weak stream of chroniton particles. It's as if the engine is on standby."

Janeway studied the screen. The strongest source of particles was in the underground chamber. But scattered near tunnels throughout the base were five live ships, including the one that took the away team.

Janeway patted Carey on the shoulder. "Nice work. It looks as if this dead base isn't quite as dead as we thought it was."

"This might be part of that solution you were looking for, Captain," Chakotay said.

"Exactly." Janeway turned to Carey. "Lieutenant, form two engineering parties of no more than four each. I want you to take apart two of the dead shuttles and discover how they work. More importantly, I want to know how we can track one through time."

Carey grinned. "I was hoping you'd want me to do that, Captain. My teams and equipment will be ready in fifteen minutes."

Janeway smiled as well. It felt good to have something to look for, a few possibilities, some real hope. Now it felt as if they were really doing something.

Paris was convinced his face was going to be bleeding by the time they got back. The wind had come up even stronger, blowing the tiny grains of sand like small flying razor blades, cutting and chipping away at any exposed skin. Even Tuvok walked with his head down and his eyes protected over his tricorder. They would check out this hunch, and then get the hell back to *Voyager*.

It took longer than they expected to reach the fifth ship. The wind was cold and sliced through Paris's thick regulation jacket. He stopped below the ship and scanned for movement. The reading he got disappointed him. Nothing moved except a metal plate inside, rocking as the ship swayed in the wind. Paris had an odd feeling about this ship, but he couldn't tell if the feeling was a warning or a push to go ahead.

"It appears to be empty," Tuvok said, studying his tricorder.

"Yep," Paris said. "So did the pavement when that ship started flying at us."

The shuttle leaned to one side slightly, but the landing gear seemed to be solid enough, and the ramp led up into a dark opening in the center. Paris walked to the bottom of the ramp.

"Let me give it a quick check," Paris said, not really wanting to climb that dark ramp. "Then we can head back."

Tuvok nodded.

Paris took a step. His breath was coming hard. That ghostly visitation on the last trip had spooked him more than he wanted to admit.

"Tuvok. Paris." The captain's voice shattered his resolve. Paris sighed with relief at the sudden reprieve. "Are you having any luck tracking our mysterious ghost?"

"No, Captain," Tuvok said.

"I'm planning on beaming down two engineering teams to work over the abandoned ships beside the live one. What size security force would you suggest to accompany them?"

"Five for each team," Tuvok said without hesitation. "Four stationed around the shuttle and one inside with the engineers."

"Fine," Janeway said. "I want you both to beam back aboard. I have another mission I need you for immediately. I'll meet you in the transporter room."

"Yes, Captain," Tuvok said.

Apparently Tuvok was anxious to be off the surface too. Paris glared at the ship. Next time. He would get to whatever bothered him next time.

Tuvok tapped his comm badge. "Two to beam up."

Paris glanced up at the ship. That was one hunch he wasn't going to get to prove. At least not at the moment.

# CHAPTER
## 15

DRICKEL HELD HIS BREATH AND LISTENED TO THE VOICES OF the Planet-Hoppers outside the ship. He tried to make out the words, but he could barely hear their voices. The wind muffled the sound and broke it apart. The thick hull of the shuttle didn't help either. He kept his finger on his personal transporter in case the Planet-Hoppers came in the door.

Before they had arrived he had managed to push the heavy metal ceiling plate off his shoulders, but the weight of it still pinned his hips and legs to the floor. With his arms free he had done a quick check of his injuries. Beside some bruises, he had a badly sprained right shoulder and a possible concussion.

All in all, he had been very lucky. When he got back he would consider requesting a regulation requiring two Watchmen to respond to alarms.

Of course, if he got back, he would prove again to himself that he really didn't need an assistant.

The wind died for a moment and the voices suddenly sounded louder. The loneliness he had felt in the caverns returned, along with a sense of helplessness. He was getting old. That was the only explanation. Early in the Watchman's job he would have welcomed a challenge like this.

If the Planet-Hoppers made it to the top of the ramp, they would see the light from his lamp. They wouldn't be able to see the lamp itself, because it and his bag were shielded, but they'd see the light. And from there it wouldn't take them long to find him under the metal plate.

He pulled his scanner off his belt and checked to see if it was broken. Luckily it wasn't. But should he use it and risk the chance that they might be able to trace the scan? Or should he simply wait?

He waited, and kept his finger on the transporter button.

If they came up the ramp, he would transport out. They'd find the lamp and maybe the bag, but not much else.

He strained to listen for more voices, but only the wind and the sound of his heart filled the silence.

Maybe they had gone.

Could he be that lucky?

He doubted it. This group of Planet-Hoppers didn't seem like the kind who gave up easily. And they were very sharp. He had a good fight ahead of him. He actually relished that. It had been a long time since he had had a real challenge.

So he waited, the heavy metal plate holding him pinned firmly to the deck. He could feel his legs, but not move them. He just hoped that when he got the plate off they would move.

The silence was more unnerving than the voices. When the wind jarred the shuttle, he winced, expecting the Planet-Hoppers.

But they didn't come.

After ten Real Time minutes he decided to risk a quick scan.

A second-long scan told him that the two Planet-Hoppers who had been outside the ship were gone. A three-second scan told him that no Planet-Hoppers were on the surface at all. For some reason they had all gone back to their ship.

He took a few deep breaths of the dry, dusty air. He'd been lucky that time. He hooked the scanner back to his belt, then went back to working the heavy plate. It moved a fraction of a millimeter and a sharp pain shot through his hip.

"Dammit," he said, relaxing on the floor as much as he could. Moving this off by hand was going to do nothing but hurt him more. He was going to be forced to take a chance with dropping the invisibility shields and beaming out.

He studied just exactly where he wanted to beam out to. Twenty meters out and ten down would put him on the surface outside the ship. That would be a safe enough distance.

But it would be cold.

And he would be in the wind again.

He promised himself that if the damage was worse

than he thought, he would transport to the caverns for protection and warmth. He knew that he probably wouldn't need to do that, but the promise provided incentive.

Badly needed incentive.

He would almost rather lie under the plate than face that deep cold. He was getting old.

He double-checked his equipment as best he could. Then he flicked off his invisibility screen and almost with the same movement hit the transport code. The weight of the heavy metal plate suddenly disappeared from his legs, and he found himself lying in the same position on concrete surface.

The wind seemed even colder than he expected. Hard blasts of sand hit his face and got in his mouth before he could close it. The sand tasted gritty and instantly made him thirsty.

He quickly flicked his invisibility screen back on and then made sure it was functioning properly. It was.

Now for the hard part.

He tried to stand.

He used his elbows to raise himself to a sitting position. Pain shot through his shoulder and hips. He waited until it subsided before pushing himself all the way to his feet.

The strong gusts of wind seemed to make him even more wobbly than he would have been, but both legs seemed to be working. His hip was stiff and he knew it was going to be very sore. He took a few shaking steps and was relieved to discover that he could walk.

"Good," he said. The cold wind took the word and

sucked it away before it got to his ears. Other than his shoulder, the soreness in his hip, and the bump on his head, he was fine. Definitely not injured enough to abandon the mission yet. Fifteen Real Time years ago he'd finished a three-day mission with a broken wrist and two cracked ribs from a fall down a hole. He could keep going this time.

He moved back to the wrecked shuttle and up the ramp into the cloud of dust still billowing inside. When he beamed out, the plate must have fallen to the floor, kicking up an incredible amount of dust. Even with the glowing light he could barely find the lantern and his bag. After a moment he found himself coughing and each cough jarred his sore shoulder.

He couldn't stay here. The ceiling wasn't secure, and it would take forever for the dust to settle. He needed another place to warm up, clean up, and rest until the Planet-Hoppers came back.

He had only one real option.

With his good hand he put the lantern back in his bag and picked up the bag.

Then, taking his time, he fought his way against the wind to the working ship the Planet-Hoppers had been so interested in. If he was going to guard it, he might as well use it.

The inside of the working ship was almost clean and warm compared to the one he'd just come from. He knew which ten seats of the hundred triggered the automatic time jump, so he stayed away from them.

He glanced around and sighed. This shuttle would be home for a while, at least until the Planet-Hoppers came back.

He set his bag on the seat closest to him. In here, at least, he knew the ship wouldn't come down on him. He could guard it at the same time as chase the Planet-Hoppers back into deep space. A good choice. Too bad he hadn't thought of it in the first place.

He took a cloth out of his bag and dampened it from his drinking supply, then wiped his face. It came away covered with dirt and he repeated the process three more times until he felt halfway clean.

"Now let's see if I can brace the shoulder a little." He went to work, pleased that he had been clear-headed enough to make a strong decision.

When, five minutes later, eighteen Planet-Hoppers appeared on the pavement outside the ship, he wondered just how smart his choice had been.

# CHAPTER
# 16

PARIS'S HANDS WERE JUST STARTING TO GET WARM AGAIN. An ache, bone deep, had developed in his fingers. The ache would turn to a sharp stinging pain before all the chill had left his hands. He and Tuvok had been exposed to the wind too long. The extreme-weather regulation clothing protected, but nothing except shelter could protect forever. Even though he hadn't had the chance to investigate that ship, he was glad he had come back to *Voyager*.

They were standing in the transporter room, waiting for Janeway. She had said she would be arriving shortly with their orders. Paris would have loved enough time for a quick shower and a chance to get the sand out of his ears. Some of it had worked its way into his nostrils and mouth. Every time he bit down, grains of sand ground between his teeth.

At least Janeway had provided for their nourishment. When Paris and Tuvok arrived, Ensign Hoffman had given them each covered tureens of soup. Paris's was plain tomato—after his temper tantrum the day he arrived on *Voyager,* the crew had not let him forget that he liked his tomato soup plain and hot, thank you, no mushrooms, no rice, and no Bolian-style cheese towers.

"I believe I got yours," Tuvok said, extending his soup tureen. "Tomato?"

"Very funny," Paris said.

"I am not attempting humor," Tuvok said.

"Right," Paris said. "You're trying to be polite. I know." But he didn't believe it. Some of that, he knew, was because he was still smarting from the hunch comment—and from the possibility that the comment might have been right.

The pneumatic doors hissed open and the captain came in. A strand of hair had escaped her normally neat bun and her uniform was rumpled. She probably hadn't eaten or slept since the away team disappeared.

Truth be told, he hadn't slept either. He was worried about the whole team, yes, but mostly he worried about Kim. That little guy had become like a kid brother to him, and Paris wasn't going to lose him like this.

"Gentlemen," Janeway said. "Our focus has shifted slightly." She quickly explained the discovery of chroniton particles emitting from the ships and the source of those particles in the caverns below the surface. "I'd like you to find that source and see it is usable for us if I determine we need to send a rescue team."

"If Kjanders speaks the truth," Tuvok said, "we risk losing a second away team."

"I know," Janeway said. "I can't ignore an opportunity, though, when it presents itself to me in this way. I also cannot rely on a man that none of my officers trust."

Paris winced inwardly at that. There was once a time when none of her officers trusted him. He wasn't sure how many did now. But she did, and Kim did, and, in his own way, Chakotay did. That was all that mattered. Still, Paris always felt as if he had to prove himself.

Janeway must have read the expression on his face, because she said, "I don't want you pulling any grandstand stunts. Is that understood?" She looked at Paris.

He grinned. The movement made his windburned skin crack. "At least," he said, "we'll be out of the wind."

"Captain?" Chakotay broke in on the comm. His voice sounded powerful even through a system that made most people sound tinny.

"Go ahead," Janeway said.

"That humanoid form appeared again on the planet's surface. Briefly, just like before."

"How long did it last?" Janeway asked.

"Actually, there were two appearances," Chakotay said. "One for just a fraction of a second inside a ship and the other for almost a second outside the same ship."

"Which ship?" Paris asked.

"The ship a quarter of a kilometer to the north of the original landing site."

Paris closed his eyes. His hunch had been right. If he had told the captain, they might have had some answers by now.

"Commander," Janeway said, "did you check for a transporter beam residual?"

"Captain," Tuvok said softly, "he will find our beam's residual in that location."

"Filter out the beam that originated on *Voyager*," Janeway said, glancing at Tuvok.

"One moment," Chakotay said.

"Captain," Paris said, "we were about to go into that ship just before we beamed out."

"If their ghost has transporter and cloaking abilities, Mr. Paris, I doubt you would have surprised it. More likely it was trying to set up a trap for you," Janeway said.

Then Chakotay broke in. "I found a different transporter trace than the one that *Voyager* uses. The humanoid was the same in both appearances."

"So far," Tuvok says, "it appears we are dealing with one person. I suspect our ghost works for Kjander's Control in one form or another."

"And he's trying to scare us away?" Paris asked. "That makes no sense."

"We know of at least one occasion when it worked," Tuvok said. "Neelix did tell us that Alcawell was haunted."

Janeway smiled sadly. "That he did."

"Captain," Tuvok said, "I believe that the cloaking

device our ghost uses might function in a similar fashion to a Romulan cloaking device. If that is the case, tracing it should be fairly simple."

A slight frown appeared between Janeway's eyes. It was a single line, really, and Paris had already noted that it meant Janeway was concentrating on something, her mind light-years away.

"Exactly, Mr. Tuvok," she said, finally. "I'll get right on it." She spun and hurried from the transporter room.

"Wow," Paris said. "You sure know how to excite her."

"I have observed," Tuvok said, "that she does enjoy logic."

Kjanders sank into a chair in the officers' mess. The coffee Chakotay had given him had left him jittery and full of energy. He had used that energy to explore several sections of the ship. *Voyager* was huge, and it wasn't a passenger ship, as many of the crew had been more than willing to tell him. One woman with a ridged nose, small chin, and jewelry on her ear of all places had told him that the captain would be willing to take him anywhere he wanted, but it would be a one-way trip only.

He didn't even know what these Planet-Hoppers used for money—or if they had a barter system, as Alcawell had had before time travel of necessity shut that system down.

His brilliant idea to get into a shuttle and go to the future had been a bust. Alcawell was deserted and Planet-Hopping was a frightening prospect. He hadn't expected adventure to be so difficult. Everything else had come easily for him. He had thought this would too.

One of the ensigns working the mess had remembered him and offered him more coffee. The cup cooled beside him. He stared out the windows. They provided him a display of his future—long blackness extending forever, his home planet shrinking in size the farther away from it he got.

This patriotism of his surprised him. He had thought he would have been happy to escape Alcawell. He was happy to be away from Control, but this starship wasn't much better. Their regulations just weren't as fierce. The woman monitoring one of the small stations near engineering hadn't even let him touch her computer. As if he would have done anything.

Yet.

His original plan had been to take over the ship. He had thought it would be easy. All Alcawellians were taught that Planet-Hoppers were slow and stupid. But they weren't. They weren't able to back-time to prevent a crime, but they had other methods. One of them was to build things so large that a single man couldn't take them over.

If he could get to the transporter equipment, though, he might be able to modify it and, using Caxton's theories, build a primitive time-travel machine.

Then he snorted. If he had had any real engineering ability, he wouldn't have turned to a life of crime. Engineers were the only truly free people on Alcawell.

He had always flunked those tests. His tests had continually shown him to be bureaucratic material and nothing else.

His only chance to remain on this ship—and to get time to learn how to use it—was to do as he had heard Kes had done. He had to make himself so useful that they couldn't get rid of him. But what skills did he have? He was a good thief. He was able to get himself out of tight situations, and he was agile.

Otherwise, he was bureaucrat material, and what place needed another bureaucrat?

Finally he sipped the tepid liquid and wrinkled his nose. Still too bitter. But he kind of liked the jitters the coffee gave him. With more energy, he would be able to explore more.

"I knew I would find you here." Chakotay's voice boomed across the room. Kjanders closed his eyes. More questions. If he had wanted questions, he would have let Control catch him before he left Real Time Period 889.

A chair scraped across the floor, then groaned as Chakotay sat. "Discovered that coffee was to your taste, huh?"

Kjanders suppressed a sigh and opened his eyes. "I like its effects. You didn't tell me it's a drug."

"A minor stimulant," Chakotay said. Then he peered into Kjanders's cup. "Well, maybe not so minor with all that sugar you've poured in there."

Kjanders picked up the cup, feeling a bit defensive about its contents. The sugar was the only thing that made the stuff taste good. "I take it this is not a social visit."

Chakotay shook his head. "We're sending a team into the past. We need to know from you what to expect and what to avoid."

Kjanders moved so quickly the coffee ran down the front of his suit. The brown stain against the brilliant blue looked faintly disgusting. "That's insane," he said.

"We understand that travel within Periods is a serious crime," Chakotay said. "We just want to get our people in and out without getting caught."

"They'll catch you," Kjanders said. "They always do."

"Control seems all-powerful," Chakotay said. "If they're that powerful, why haven't they caught you?"

"Because this place is empty," Kjanders said. "That's why I got away with it in the first place. I thought maybe they didn't know where I was, that I got lost in the system somehow, but no. They knew I was coming here and they knew I wouldn't survive. So why waste all that energy and back-time just for little old me."

A bitterness he hadn't known he felt came through as he spoke. He brushed at the coffee stain, but couldn't get it off with his hands.

Chakotay handed him a cloth from a nearby table. The cloth smelled of vinegar. "How can we make certain our people get lost in the system?"

Kjanders mopped at the stain. The combined smell of vinegar and coffee reminded his stomach that it didn't like the new liquid. "Look, Commander, let me explain it to you in this fashion. Say you're Control and I wanted to escape from you. I jump up and run out the door, or transport to the surface, or even jump back in time. Anything. And I am successful at my getaway."

Chakotay nodded.

"So, you as Control declare a Time Alarm and simply short-jump a force back to the moment I am running out the door. They would greet me there and my escape would never take place."

Chakotay sat back in his chair, his hands folded over his belly. He was obviously thinking and Kjanders let him think.

After a moment he sat forward again. "So the only chance of success would be to stay out of Control's hands and their attention. Right?"

"Correct," Kjanders said. "But the problem is that your crew members are in Control's hands, so even if you did rescue them, the rescue attempt would always be stopped. Always. Once Control has you, you can never, ever get away."

Chakotay pushed himself to his feet. "There has to be something we are missing," Chakotay said. "Some way to rescue them."

Kjanders kept mopping. The stain had woven its way into the fibers. If this stuff was so difficult on clothing, what was it doing to his insides?

"Kjanders," Chakotay said softly, "if there is a way, and you happen to think of it, I am sure the captain would be very pleased."

Kjanders grimaced, directing the look at the stain, even though it was really for Chakotay. Finally, the idea he had been playing with had presented itself—a way to become indispensable. Only the way to become indispensable was the way to get himself killed.

He sighed. He wouldn't help them with this one. He couldn't. He set the cloth down. "Give it up, Chakotay. You can't help your people. You'll only lose more people."

"No wonder your Control became so strong," Chakotay snapped. "You people give up before even trying."

"No," Kjanders said. "We just value our lives."

# CHAPTER

# 17

IT WAS NOT A GOOD DAY TO DIE.

Torres used to hate that phrase of her mother's. Her mother, staunch Klingon that she was, sometimes went into a difficult situation saying, *Today is a good day to die.* And little B'Elanna never agreed. There never was a good day to die.

And if there had been, today would not have been it.

Her pacing seemed to have caught on. Kim was pacing too. They were stalking the room like caged animals. She knew each centimeter of this place, from its neon green carpet to its puce furniture. No windows, only pink walls in the main quarters, lots of red and chrome in the kitchen and bathroom.

Neelix was sitting on the floor. He had dug the blossoms she had picked off the trees out of the garbage and was pulling them apart, petal by petal.

Their stench filled the room, which was probably why Torres was thinking of her mother again, but she didn't have the heart to tell Neelix to quit.

"She loves me," Kim said as Neelix pulled one petal.

Torres stopped and looked at him. Had Kim finally gone over the edge?

"She loves me not," Kim said as Neelix plucked another petal.

"Whatever are you doing?" Torres asked.

Kim's grin was sheepish. "It's an old child's game. We played it on Earth. When there's one petal left you know—is it a 'she loves me' or a 'she loves me not'? It should be 'Will they kill me' or 'Will they kill me not.'"

"Will they kill me," Neelix recited as he pulled one petal. "Will they kill me not?"

"Stop it!" Torres reached down, grabbed the offensive blooms, and took them into the kitchen. This time she put them in a compactor unit and turned it on. The scent of wilted petals filled the kitchen like a bad perfume.

Neelix sighed. "I suppose that really wasn't funny."

"I don't think any of this is really funny," Kim said.

"Neither do I." Torres stood in the archway between the kitchen and living quarters. "And it feels wrong to me to wait for some bureaucrat to get us through a system that doesn't care about us at all."

"But what can we do?" Kim said. "We already saw how they back-time to get to us, often at the point where we just thought of the action."

"And," Neelix said, "as much faith as I have in your

wonderful Captain Janeway, I don't believe even she can find us in this horrible place."

"If she even tried," Kim said, "she would probably run into the same problems we did."

"My," Torres said, "aren't we a cheery bunch?"

The other two looked away. Neelix wiped off his hands and stood. Kim flopped on a nearby couch.

"I've been thinking," Torres said. "Rawlik is right. They'll catch us no matter what. Unless we succeed."

"What?" Neelix asked.

Kim sat up. "Exactly," he said. "If we succeed and get back to our own time, they won't back up time to get us."

"There are days when explanations seem clear," Neelix muttered, "and days when I believe I left my brain in its jar beside my bed."

Both Torres and Kim turned to him with surprise.

"Figuratively speaking," he said.

"We're going to have to try," Torres said. "Even if we fail, at least we will have known that we tried."

"Good point," Neelix said. "I hope."

She looked at him. "Can you draw the guard in the hall closer to the door?"

"Can I draw the guard closer to the door?" he said in a chiding way. "Just watch."

"Wait!" Torres said. "Let me explain this idea. I'll need your help too, Ensign. I think the only hope we have is to get back to the smaller time shuttle we came in and catch a ride back. If we make it that far, I assume we've made it."

"That makes sense," Kim said. "If they're going to stop us, they'll do it before we get on the shuttle."

"And if we take the guard as a hostage," Neelix said, "then they'd have to stop us before we got to him. Right?"

"Right," Torres said and for the first time a faint ray of hope cut through the gloom in her mind. If they did manage to get to the guard, then a hostage might do the trick. "Let's move. Neelix, do your stuff. Get him close and I'll grab him." Her blood was racing at the thought of battle. This felt right. They were taking action.

"With pleasure," he said. He headed for the door, moving with a purposeful little march. When he grabbed the handle, the door burst open. Neelix had to stagger back and away as Rawlik and two orange suits came in.

"Damn," Torres whispered.

"Nice timing," Neelix said under his breath, then glanced at Torres. "That wasn't accidental?"

Torres shook her head. All the adrenaline pumping through her body suddenly had nowhere to go. She started forward, but the orange suits trained weapons on her.

"Don't, B'Elanna," Rawlik said. "Last time you got shot up pretty good."

"Then why didn't you back-time to get me?" she snapped.

"We did. You broke both the guards' jaws before we could restrain you. We decided that maybe reason would prevent bloodshed."

"Funny," she said, "we were hoping that would work with your people."

"I've got to admit," Rawlik said, "we've never had prisoners as determined and creative as you three."

"Thanks," Neelix said. "I think."

Kim clasped his hands behind his back. "So," he said, "how far did we get on our first attempt?"

"Almost to the time shuttle with the guard as hostage." Rawlik paused and looked directly at Torres. "You know this new violation won't help your chances much in the morning."

"Did we really have much chance anyway?" Torres asked.

"No," Rawlik said. "But all this effort is not inspiring to the council. I'll still see what I can do."

"Thank you," Torres said. She worked hard to keep the sarcasm out of her voice. The energy was still flowing through her. Another few hours of pacing might get rid of it. "We'll wait here."

She dropped down into a thick chair and put her feet up, pretending to be unconcerned. She'd made up her mind. When they came to take her to her death tomorrow she'd die fighting. She would go out in such a way as to make her Klingon mother proud.

Neelix sat down in the chair beside her as Rawlik motioned for the guards to take up positions on both sides of the door. Then Rawlik nodded to Torres and left without a word.

"Well," Kim said. "I guess we gave it a good try."

"I must have been brilliant," Neelix said. "I only wish I could remember it."

When the transporter beam released him, Paris let out a sigh. No wind, and relative warmth—at least zero degrees Celsius, which was balmy compared to the surface. What a relief.

He had arrived before Tuvok, something Ensign Hoffman had warned them about, considering the layers of rock and equipment the signal would have to penetrate.

Tuvok materialized a half second behind him, lantern already lit. Tiny dust motes floated in the air around them, apparently disturbed by Paris's first movement.

"Wow," Paris said.

This had obviously been a huge control center, with workstations and paths through them. Hundreds of people must have worked here at once. But now everything had a smooth, gray look to it as if covered with dirty snow. The air was bone dry, but at least the wind wasn't cutting his skin down here.

"Move slowly," Tuvok said, pointing downward.

Paris glanced down. A thick layer of fine, light dust flowed over the top of his shoes. The dust was still settling from his first involuntary movement.

"We will have to be very careful in here," Tuvok said. "Each movement could create a dust storm. Step lightly and spread out so that we don't cover the other person." Tuvok glanced at his tricorder and then said, "This way."

They headed off to the right. Paris took slow, medium steps. After ten feet, he wished for the wind.

With each step, no matter how softly taken, the dust would swirl into the air in billowing clouds. He couldn't avoid breathing the stuff. He finally reached into his kit, and removed a mask. Tuvok did the same.

Then Paris got out his lantern. In this dust they were going to need them both.

Both men waited for the dust to settle, but most of it just stayed in the air swirling with the faint currents their movement had caused.

"Stay ahead of it," Tuvok said, and they started walking again.

Paris didn't even want to breathe hard. The stuff coated him and stuck to any moisture. He was glad that the cavern wasn't hot. If he were sweating the stuff would coat him like glue.

"Wow, this is some dust, isn't it?" He tried to sound casual, but he doubted Tuvok was fooled.

"The tricorder says so," Tuvok said. "Nothing harmful in the particles. They are just inconvenient."

Which was, apparently, the Vulcan way of saying damn annoying.

They finally settled on a pace that would allow them to stay just barely ahead of the clouds their movements were making. "Don't stop fast," Paris said.

He found himself thinking of ways to avoid the dust instead of ways to help Kim and the others. That annoyed him even more.

Tuvok indicated ahead. "Fresh prints leading away from the time machine and toward that tunnel."

Paris carefully slowed down as he neared the prints. He didn't want to disturb them. "They could be new or they could be twenty years old. It's impossible to tell since the air doesn't move down here."

"Not impossible," Tuvok said. "Notice that the corners of the prints are firm, not rounded and pulled down by gravity. These prints are recent. They lead to a tunnel which is located beneath the shuttle that took the first away team. Our ghost's first appearance on our equipment occurred when he transported to the surface directly over that tunnel."

Paris nodded. "So, as we figured, our ghost wears boots."

The both turned and slowly made their way toward the time shuttle. It was down a very dusty hall. They had to cover the distance of the hall side by side, shoulders almost touching to keep the dust from choking them. They weren't so lucky with the doors and Paris ended up following Tuvok through gray clouds that even his lantern had trouble penetrating.

By the time they reached the small room, they were caked in gray dust. Tuvok looked like a ghost himself. The gray leached the color from his uniform, and lodged on his skin and hair. His mask, initially white, was now gray and probably as useless as Paris's had become. Paris's nose was totally blocked and he could taste the grit against his teeth. God only knew what it was doing to his eyes.

"An individual time shuttle," Tuvok said as he stood and stared at the small machine off one side of the room. Prints in the dust led away from the machine. "This area here—" He pointed the tricorder at where a workstation once was. "—used to control this machine and probably still does three hundred thousand years in the past."

Paris moved slowly closer to the shuttle. "So this shuttle must be set for automatic return. When our ghost finishes his mission, he gets in and goes home."

"That would seem logical."

They both studied the machine. Paris could find no obvious means of propulsion, although the thing was emitting a thin, steady stream of chroniton particles.

Finally, Tuvok tapped his comm badge. *"Voyager?"*

"Go ahead, Mr. Tuvok," Captain Janeway's voice answered. Even through the comm badge it filled the small room with authority. Paris looked up, half expecting a cloud of dust to rise in reaction to the strength of the captain's voice.

"We have found the time shuttle. It appears to be built for one or two people. It has obviously been used by someone in the very near past."

"Is there any evidence of that person nearby?" Janeway asked.

"Footprints," Paris said. "But we didn't expect to find our ghost here. It's still got to be on the surface. Have the teams on the surface had any spectral visitations?"

"Not yet," Janeway said. "But they just got there less than ten minutes ago."

"Captain," Tuvok said. "After viewing this area, I have an idea on how to capture our ghost. Have the transporter room lock in the coordinates of this room so we can beam directly back here when we need to."

"Thank you," Paris said under his breath. He didn't much like the thought of another trek through the dust of that huge cavern and those halls.

"Then beam us directly to the landing party," Tuvok said.

Paris moaned. A shower and a little more tomato soup would have been nice first. Ah, well, better to get filthy all in one trip. That way if they had to use engine-room grade scrapers to get the dirt off, they would only have to do it once.

"Stand by," Janeway said.

A moment later the transporter beam took them from the murky room to the high wind and blowing sand of the surface. The dirt from Paris's mask blew into his eyes. With a quick, impatient gesture, he ripped the mask off and let the wind take it. Then he winced as the sand cut into the tiny unhealed cuts on his cheeks.

"I'm beginning to really hate this place," Paris said.

# CHAPTER
## 18

DRICKEL FINISHED BINDING HIS ARM SO THAT HE WOULDN'T jar his injured shoulder. He made certain he had enough flexibility to allow the use of his right hand. He had taken a special powder for his headache and pain—one that allowed him to think clearly, but that dulled the pain. He half hoped the powder would dull the effects of the wind as well.

The voices outside were businesslike and insistent. Drickel had monitored the new arrivals for a few minutes before tending his arm. For once, the Planet-Hoppers weren't interested in this ship, but in the ships beside it. At first he had thought that a good coincidence. Then he realized they were taking the ships apart, trying to see how they worked.

Judging by the sophistication of the transporter devices and the calm with which old Pointed Ears had faced Drickel earlier, these Planet-Hoppers just might figure everything out. Which gave Drickel only a short time to medicate himself, bind his arm, and prepare for his next show.

He decided against threatening the Planet-Hoppers, at least for the moment. He would put on a great floating display, and if that didn't work he would pursue the weakest link with something sharp and shiny. Watchman Regulation Code 3,765.41, Section 01, stated that no interloper could be hurt without just cause. The just-cause clause had recently been superseded by Code 3,765.41, Section 01.1A, and its language was confusing. He still didn't know if he could cause injury or, if he did, whether he would be allowed to back-time to prevent it.

Sometimes a man had to operate on guesswork with all these regulations. Considering what he was up against here, he didn't want to mess with any changes at all. Besides, to back-time he would have to get special dispensation (Watchman Regulation Code 00001.18, Section 99.32B), and sometimes that dispensation took a month of Real Time hearings.

He was having too much fun matching wits with these Planet-Hoppers to interrupt it now with special hearings.

Drickel grabbed his bag with his good hand, made certain he had all the equipment he needed, and double-checked his invisibility cloak. Then he moved down the hall and out of the shuttle.

The wind seemed even colder than it had before, and the sand was blowing so hard it actually made lines across his vision. He had to squint to see clearly.

He got to the bottom of the ramp and studied the scene. A man in a dull yellow and black uniform stood weapon at ready, his back to the wind. He seemed to be guarding the north side of one of the wrecks. Drickel assumed that was one of the wrecks being worked on. Another guard stood in a sheltered location to the west, another to the east, and Drickel could make out a fourth to the south of the same wreck. Four other guards stood in similar positions around a second wreck. On that ship, Drickel could see other Planet-Hoppers ripping the hull and moving the plates aside.

This was clearly not scavenging work. This was serious investigation.

Drickel stood beside the ramp, as far out of the wind as he could get. He used his sensors to determine what he was up against.

There were five more Planet-Hoppers inside each ship, but only one had a weapon.

"An awful lot of firepower," he said to himself. "I bet that's all for me." He laughed as the wind carried his voice away. They'd never catch him. He was the best from the Back Room. No one had ever been able to keep pace with him.

No one.

Not in over two hundred and forty successfully completed missions.

These people wouldn't find him either. They showed their nervousness through the level of firepower they had brought with them. That many guards and weapons meant the Planet-Hoppers were afraid of him. Or at the very least, worried. And that was exactly what he wanted them to be.

Worried.

He used his good arm to shift his bag to his shoulder. Now they were in for a real show. He had twenty antigravity pads and countless smaller antigravity disks. He'd see how these Planet-Hoppers would act with five old wrecks in the air at once.

Keeping his face as covered as he could from the wind, he walked across the open area. He still favored his bruised hip—the powder had dulled the pain but not taken it away—and the wind was stronger, actually a force he had to fight. He dug out some of the pads as he walked. When he reached the wreck he had used in the first show, he carefully placed the pads in the exact same spots on the underside. This wreck was right beside one of the ships the Planet-Hoppers were working on. A guard was using it for a sort of shelter from the wind as he stood duty.

After placing the pads, Drickel walked up behind the guard and tugged slightly on his right ear. The guy spun, weapon at ready. Drickel held up his hands, pretending he was captured, as the guy looked around wildly, finally shaking his head, and scratching his ear before returning his attention to his duty.

Drickel yanked on the guard's ear again and then moved on to the next ship laughing as the guard frantically searched for something he couldn't see.

As Drickel placed four more pads on the underside of another wreck, something caught his eye. Two men shimmered in the last sparkles of a transporter beam.

They were beaming into an open area near the working time shuttle.

The men were covered with dirt—their uniforms were gray—and they wore masks over their faces. The wind instantly blew the dirt off them. The first man ripped his mask off and let the wind take it. The other man took off his mask and calmly folded it into his pocket.

Old Pointed Ears and his pale companion.

Drickel's stomach twisted. They had obviously been into the old Control caverns. If they saw his footprints they would know he wasn't a ghost. Then an even worse thought struck him. What if they had found the shuttle?

For the second time on this mission he felt a sense of urgency. If he didn't move fast he might lose this one. And he didn't want to think about what exactly that meant.

He limped to the third wreck and hurriedly placed the pads on the proper locations. For the moment three floating wrecks would have to be enough. He just didn't have the time to do all five.

When he finished, he stood partially under the last shuttle. The sand stung like tiny chunks of ice as he pulled the remote control out of his bag and keyed in the first ship. It slowly floated three meters off the ground.

The guard under it yelled and ran out into the open, his weapon at ready. His eyes were wide, and he continued shouting until the others turned to watch.

"So far so good," Drickel said to himself.

Quickly Drickel switched on the control for the

second ship and floated a full ten meters off the pavement. The winds at that height were stronger, and the ship bucked once. Drickel adjusted the pads, then held the ship steady.

Its broken ramp banged against the underside of the shuttle, sending resounding booms floating off on the wind. Two guards pointed to the new wreck and ran into the open area.

Pointed Ears took out his sensor and calmly studied the wreck. His pale companion watched for a moment, hands on his hips and a bemused expression on his face, before pulling out his sensors and moving in the opposite direct from Pointed Ears. Both men aimed their sensors at the floating shuttles, then swept the sensors around the area, obviously trying to find him.

"Go ahead," Drickel said aloud. "Try to find me if you can."

He keyed in the third set of pads on the shuttle over his head and let it lift two meters up. It too wavered slightly in the wind but held steady, its ramp still touching the concrete about two meters from Drickel.

Now the guards appeared really confused.

They were surrounded by three wrecks floating without reason. They seemed disoriented, but after a moment Drickel became impressed by their control and discipline. All had their weapons at ready, but not a one of them fired at the floating ships. Mostly they just watched and stayed ready.

"Tough audience," Drickel said.

He turned to see what the two men with the sensors were doing. Pointed Ears had moved closer to Drickel and was examining the shuttle floating above him. After a moment, he waved his hand toward his pale companion, indicating that the man should come closer. The pale companion nodded.

Without aiming his sensor device at anything, Pointed Ears keyed something in and then looked up, as if he expected a reaction.

And he got one.

At that very instant Pointed Ears looked up, the control in Drickel's hand sent out a faint warning light.

He glanced down. The link to all the pads had been severed, shutting them down.

He cursed and ran, forgetting the pain in his hip.

A groan echoed above him as a gust of wind hit the shuttle at the same time as the antigravity cut off.

By the time the landing gear hit the ground, Drickel had taken one full running step. But those old stubby lander legs had never been made to come down so quickly from such a height. It wouldn't have been able to take the weight of the shuttle dropped from two meters in the air when it was brand new.

His only hope was that he would get out from under it.

He did, but not the way he wanted.

He had taken another step before the landing leg farthest from him snapped like a thousand guns discharging at once. Pieces of the landing gear bombarded him like shrapnel.

He felt as if he were running underwater.

Time felt as if it had slowed, even though he knew it hadn't.

One more step.

One more step and he'd be out from under the wreck. He took half the step when the landing gear closest to him shattered.

He felt the concussion like a bomb going off next to him.

Then the impact hit him, knocking the breath out of his body and sending him into the air.

Flying.

Flying.

Flying away from the crashing shuttle.

Mercifully the blackness took him before he hit the ground.

# CHAPTER
## 19

CAPTAIN JANEWAY STOOD BESIDE ENSIGN HOFFMAN IN THE transporter room. Hoffman's able fingers were bringing the last of the away team up: Carey, Tuvok, and Paris. The others had already been beamed aboard—one to sickbay. The holographic doctor had complained about the lack of warning.

As the last three members materialized, Janeway understood why Tuvok suggested that she meet them in the transporter room instead of the bridge. Carey looked fine, a little dirty from working on the old shuttle and a bit windblown, but relatively healthy.

At least compared to Paris and Tuvok.

They looked as if they'd just crawled out of a cave-in. They were covered in dirt. It was so thick on their uniforms the color was gone, and their faces were smeared with it. Only their eyes were visible, and

Paris's whites were so red, they looked like they were bleeding, while Tuvok's inner eyelid was more than half closed.

"I trust nothing happened in the caverns," Janeway said.

"No," Paris said, "if you don't count being assaulted by millions of years of accumulated dust."

"I believe the accumulation appeared to be only a hundred thousand years' worth," Tuvok said. "I doubt we would have been able to walk in——"

"Anyway, Captain," Paris said, "we're fine. Which is more than I can say for Ensign Berggren."

"Sickbay says he was cut by flying shrapnel," Janeway says. "He'll be fine. But I would like to know exactly what happened."

"Apparently," Tuvok said, "our ghost decided that we needed to see more than one flying ship. It was using antigravity pads run by a remote control. I blocked the signal and the ships fell back to the ground."

"The crashes were spectacular," Paris said. "And so loud I swear you could have heard them up here."

Tuvok ignored him. Janeway suppressed a smile. It appeared Paris was interrupting just to annoy Tuvok. It wouldn't work. Tuvok did not annoy.

"If we shift through the wreckage we shall be able to recover the devices," Tuvok said. "I am concerned that we will not be able to find our ghost. Logically, it should have tried something else after the crashes. But, although we remained on the surface a good ten minutes longer, nothing happened."

"Do you have a hypothesis, Mr. Tuvok?"

"I believe it may be injured, even dead."

Ensign Hoffman made a small sound beside Janeway. Janeway glanced at her. Hoffman and Torres had been working on special projects in Engineering. Apparently they had become friends. Hoffman knew, as everyone else did, that the ghost was their best chance of discovering how to bring the away team back.

"Go on," Janeway said.

"I traced the signal emitting from the remote control to a location under one of the crashed shuttles."

"Any sign of a body?"

"No," Tuvok said. "But it may be injured and close and we would never see it."

"If the ghost was under that ship as it fell," Paris said, "it would have taken a very amazing person to get out. It was only a few meters in the air."

"So how do you propose finding this ghost?"

"Heat, Captain," Tuvok said. "An injured person would not move much. The body will build up a heat signature, which I might be able to trace."

"If the ghost is dead, that won't work." Carey spoke for the first time.

"I know," Tuvok said. "But if it is dead, we do not need to find it."

"Let's try," Janeway said. "Paris, are you able to help him?"

"I am," he said. Janeway almost laughed at the look in his eyes. She could tell that the last thing he wanted to do was return to that planet's surface. But as long as Kim was missing, he'd go back as often as it took. It was one of the many traits about Paris she admired.

"Good," she said. She turned to Carey as Tuvok stepped to one side and tapped his comm badge to secure the right equipment. "How is the study of the wrecks coming?"

"It was going fine until the excitement. Nothing definite yet on what makes the time travel work, but we are stockpiling the metal plates from the interior of the ship on Hangar Deck Two. Those plates can be used very nicely as raw materials for parts."

"Good," she said. "Keep at it. Regroup your teams and beam back down. I want you continuing on that line. But help Tuvok and Paris anytime they need it. Finding that ghost is a priority. Understood?"

"Understood, Captain."

"We are ready," Tuvok said.

The two men stepped back up on the transporter platform. While Carey moved off to quickly put his engineering teams back together. Paris put his hands up to cover his eyes from the blowing sand.

Tuvok stood there stoically.

"Good luck," she said as the beam took them. She hoped they found that ghost. She didn't want to rely on Kjanders for everything.

They hadn't slept. Torres, Kim, and Neelix had stayed awake ever since Rawlik left the last time, eating pieces of the snack he had brought them and discussing options. There had to be a way to beat this time-travel system. Torres just hadn't found it yet.

She had once told a friend that she could find the loopholes in any bureaucracy. Only two had thwarted her: Starfleet and now Alcawell. Starfleet had allowed her to leave—not peaceably, since that was not her way—but she was still able to continue her life.

Alcawell was determined to take even that.

Rawlik had become their only hope.

Things had become pretty hopeless if their only hope was the chief bureaucrat in a bureaucracy that prided itself on its adherence to rules.

"I wish we had windows," Kim said. "Rawlik said he would be talking to the council in the morning, but how are we to know when morning is? We don't even know if this planet has a twenty-four-hour day."

"Or if they continually add hours at the end of each day to write more rules," Neelix said. He leaned back on the couch. "I didn't even say a proper good-bye to Kes. I thought I would be back soon enough. It shows that one should always expect the unexpected."

"That's a cliché where I come from," Kim said.

"Clichés are clichés because they have a level of wisdom," Neelix said.

"Clichés are clichés," Torres said, "because people use them in the wrong circumstances."

"I would wager that particular cliché is not a cliché on Alcawell," Neelix said.

"No," Kim said. "Here they anticipate the unexpected and thwart it."

Torres glanced at Kim. The fear seemed to have left him. Long hours with nothing to do often did that for folks. And she had to remember how strong he was. She had faced death with him before. Then the odds had seemed long too.

Still, they had found a solution.

Here, the solutions always created more problems.

The door opened and Rawlik entered carrying their breakfast tray. Torres wrinkled her nose at it as he set it on a footstool. Several pastries that looked like mashed beets mixed with bright red food dye and three glasses of a purple beverage the color of Rawlik's assistant's hair.

Torres ignored the food for a moment, even though her stomach was growling. "Are the appeals finished?"

Rawlik picked up one of the pastries and took a bite. He chewed and swallowed before answering her. "The council is still in session. I went in front of them a hour ago Real Time and pleaded your case. Breakfast?" He offered the tray to Neelix.

"Well," Neelix said, taking a pastry and a glass. "This won't be our last meal if the council remains in session all day."

Kim took his glass as well. "You know," he said to Rawlik, "it would be better if you stocked the kitchen like Neelix said. Then you wouldn't have to break from your arguments and serve us."

"I'm done arguing," Rawlik said.

Neelix took a tentative sip of the liquid. "It's sweet," he said with surprise.

Torres took a glass as Kim sipped his.

"It doesn't really taste familiar," Kim said.

Torres drank. On the contrary, the drink tasted very familiar. "My mother used to make something similar," she said. "A Klingon specialty called Vleq. I always called it Yuk. She served it hot, though."

"We can warm it for you," Rawlik said.

Torres shook her head. "No need. I would rather hear about the proceedings. How soon will we know?"

"Soon," Rawlik said. He paced around the room, following the same path Torres had.

Neelix and Kim hadn't touched their pastries, but they had both finished the drink. Torres finished hers as well. It was just like Vleq. Even though it was sweet, it didn't completely quench a thirst. It only promised to do so. The idea of pastries after a drink that sweet made her vaguely nauseated.

"If the council decides against us," she said, "where do we appeal?"

"There is no appeal," Rawlik said quietly. "The council is the highest authority. I am afraid that now we can only wait."

"Well," Neelix said, stretching out on the sofa, "I have learned that the best way to wait is to nap. I've always been fond of naps. Sometimes Kes says I nap too much. . . ."

His voice trailed away.

Kim was nodding. "Yeah," he said. "A nap sounds good."

"Don't nap," Torres said to Neelix. "When you nap, we always get in trouble."

Then the exhaustion hit her. Only it didn't feel like real exhaustion. It felt—more welcoming.

*Don't nap. When you nap—*

Then somewhere in the back of her mind she realized what was going on.

She launched herself at Rawlik, but the two guards had already moved into position. "You poisoned us!"

Rawlik nodded. "There was no other way."

"The council?"

He actually looked sad. "I'm sorry."

She yanked herself out of the guards' grasp. The movement made her dizzy. "I was going to go out fighting," she said. Her words were slurred. "Take a few of you scummy time freaks with me."

Rawlik nodded, and she could barely see his face at this point. "You did," he said. "You were the only people in the history of this culture to cause four Time Alarms."

She didn't care about that. She fell to her knees beside the sofa and grabbed Neelix's shoulders. "Wake up!" she said. She had heard somewhere that drugs didn't always work if people stayed awake. But his body was heavy. He wasn't moving. "Wake up!"

She turned to Kim. "Wake up!"

His eyes were partially open. She couldn't tell if he was breathing.

She pushed herself to her feet. "I'm still going to go out fighting," she said. She flailed at Rawlik. He caught her wrists. He wouldn't have been able to do that if she had been up to full strength.

"You already fought. You and your friends killed five of my men and wounded five others, including a council member, before we back-timed for this solution."

She jerked in his grasp. The dizziness was growing. "That's supposed to make me happy?"

"I'm very sorry," Rawlik said.

"You know," she said, her voice seeming far, far away, "we only wanted to go home."

He eased her back to the sofa. She tried to move, but she couldn't.

She wanted to tell him that he would regret this for the rest of his life.

She wanted to leap off the sofa and break out of this hell.

Her eyes closed against her will, and she fought, moving the fight inward, where it had always been.

She had fought her dual nature and survived. She would fight this.

She did fight this—

Until she couldn't anymore.

# CHAPTER

# 20

PARIS WOULD NEVER THINK OF SAND AS BENIGN AGAIN. THE wind was even harsher than before, the chill so deep that his thermal gloves couldn't keep it out. The sand lacerated his jacket and would bite into his uniform soon. Someone once told him that they made glass out of sand. Now he believed it.

He and Tuvok were moving equipment. Carey had joined them and then gone to check on the crews that followed them back down to the surface.

Tuvok was convinced that the ghost was sophisticated enough that a tricorder alone wouldn't pick up the ghost's body heat. Tuvok's argument was that if the ghost had initially given off body heat, it would have registered right away. So he brought an elaborate sensor designed, Tuvok said, for special space work.

It would do here, or so Tuvok claimed.

Paris was tired of claims. He just wanted action. He wanted to find that ghost before it died, before he lost his opportunity ever to see Kim again.

Tuvok motioned to Paris and together they moved the dishlike sensor. It wasn't actually a sensor in and of itself. The job of sensor would be filled by Tuvok's tricorder. The dish gathered the heat signals and amplified them to the tricorder. The problem was that the dish, which was a meter and a half across, needed a certain amount of steadiness to get any readings at all. Paris wondered how anything was going to stay steady in this wind, especially a dish.

Tuvok finished linking his tricorder and the dish. Paris did not like the look in Tuvok's eye.

"Hold it as steady as you can," Tuvok said. He was actually using their comm link so that they wouldn't have to shout over the howling wind. "We will try the area around where we found the control first."

Paris sat down on the ground and half wrapped his body around the round metal dish. He stretched out his legs to serve as an anchor and let his back work as a wind foil. Then he nodded to indicate his readiness. "You know," he said, "I'm sure if you had asked, Engineering would have given you a sturdy tripod. It wouldn't complain about the wind or the sand or even the wretched cold."

"This will only take a moment, Lieutenant."

"A tripod wouldn't care how long it took. A tripod—"

"Would sheer in this kind of gale force." Tuvok studied the readout for a moment. "Move it slightly to the left."

Paris scooted his butt and legs slightly and again braced himself. The pavement was made of ice, and the sand had gone down the waistband of his pants. The feeling the little rock crystals left was not pleasant.

"A tripod," he said, "would—"

"A tripod would have the sense to remain quiet," Tuvok said. His words were flat and unemotional, but Paris sensed a well of emotion behind them. Perhaps he was just imagining that emotion. Perhaps Tuvok's statement was entirely logical given the circumstances.

Perhaps not.

Perhaps Paris had finally gotten through those thick Vulcan defenses.

Paris took a deep breath and fought to make himself relax a little against the wind, not fight it so much. This was going to be a very long job if they had to scan the entire area like this. Paris stretched out his aching back for a moment, then adjusted the dish scanner another degree and braced it again.

Tuvok studied the readings for a moment, then looked up at where the dish was pointed, then studied the readings again. "I did not ask you to move the dish," Tuvok said. "But I am glad you did. Our ghost exists."

He continued to stare at the tricorder as he ran toward the edge of the crashed ship. It took a moment for Paris to put the dish facedown so the wind wouldn't kick it around before he could climb to his feet and follow.

Thirty meters away Tuvok slowed and then started

easing forward. At about the same moment that Paris caught him, Tuvok's foot obviously struck something and Tuvok leaned down, his hands moving over an invisible object.

Paris moved in closer and knelt down on the hard pavement across from Tuvok. Now that he was looking, he could see the sand building up small drifts around something on the ground. There was no distortion at all. Their ghost had one of the best cloaking devices he had ever seen.

He extended his hand and found cloth. His hand hovered over what appeared to be emptiness, but on close examination, he realized that the blowing sand avoided a space about the size of a human body. He moved his hand until he found what felt like a human arm.

"He is still alive," Tuvok shouted against the wind.

Relief flooded him, but he blocked it as best he could. Just because the ghost lived didn't mean that they could find Kim and the others.

He tapped his comm badge. *Voyager.* Three to beam up directly to sickbay."

"Sir, my instruments only show two," Hoffman's voice said barely loud enough to be heard over the wind.

Paris pulled off his badge and stuck it on the ghost. The badge floated in midair. "My comm badge is now on the other body. Now engage."

The transporter cut off the wind as if it had shut off bad music that someone had been playing far too loud. As they materialized on the floor of sickbay,

Paris suddenly discovered parts of his body the wind had numbed and the sand had abused.

The sickbay was empty except for Ensign Berggren asleep on one of the bunks. His hands were bandaged, his mouth was open, and he was snoring slightly. Apparently their arrival hadn't disturbed him.

"Initiate emergency medical program," Tuvok said.

Doc Zimmerman appeared instantly. "What seems to be the problem?" His voice was flat and almost annoyed.

"We have a seriously injured person here," Paris said.

"Really?" Doc Zimmerman said, looking around.

Tuvok ignored Doc Zimmerman and tapped his comm badge. "Captain, we have our ghost on board in sickbay."

"On my way." Janeway's curt response filled the room.

"Ghost?" Doc Zimmerman said. "I am only programmed to work on corporeal beings."

"Can we lift him up on a table?" Paris said.

Tuvok nodded.

Paris slid his hands underneath the ghost and got a hold as Tuvok did the same on the other side.

"There is no one between you," Doc Zimmerman said.

Tuvok glanced at Paris. "Ready?"

Paris was as ready as he was ever going to get, lifting a ghost. "Ready."

"Now," Tuvok said. Together they both lifted the solid weight of the body and moved over until they could place it on a table.

"I will review the treatments for mass hallucination," Doc Zimmerman said.

Paris grunted as he lifted. This ghost was heavy. He and Tuvok staggered under the weight.

"My psychological programming is limited. However, if you don't mind stepping over to one of the tables, I will see if your delusion has a physical basis."

As Paris eased his hands out from under the invisible body, he could feel a wide and very solid belt around the waist. "The controls might be in this belt."

Tuvok felt the air over the ghost's middle carefully, then pulled his hands back as Janeway came through the door.

She moved directly up to the table between Tuvok and Paris and looked at its empty surface. "Amazing," she said.

"Not another one," Doc Zimmerman said. He rolled his eyes.

"That it is, Captain," Tuvok said. "The shield even blocked most of the heat from the body. A very sophisticated cloaking."

"Or phasing," Janeway said.

Doc Zimmerman suddenly came forward. Apparently the talk of cloaking and phasing made him revise his assessment. "Are you telling me," he said, "that my patient is actually invisible?"

"Yes," Paris snapped. "Get to it, will you? We have no idea what condition this person is in."

"Move aside," Doc Zimmerman said. "Allow me. I'm the doctor here."

Tuvok didn't move. "The lieutenant believes that the controls might be on the ghost's belt. I agree.

However, it may be dangerous to tamper with it. We do not know what we are doing."

"Clearly," Doc Zimmerman snapped. "You are absolutely filthy. You drag an invisible patient in here and then shed dirt on it. For all I know, you could be compounding this patient's problems. Now move out of my way."

"Give them a moment, Doctor," Janeway said.

"If this patient is seriously injured," Doc Zimmerman said, "we may not have a moment."

"Why don't we just take the belt off?" Paris said.

Janeway thought for a moment. "That seems to be an acceptable risk at this time."

Paris started feeling along the lumpy, solid belt from his side until he reached what felt like a buckle. He ran his hands over it for a moment, realizing as he did that it was just a simple utility-belt-type latch. Nothing special. It was made to be released quickly, obviously in case of emergency.

"I hope you are not touching any open wounds," Doc Zimmerman said. "The risk of infection is always greater in an uncontrolled environment."

"Ready?" Paris asked, looking up at Janeway.

"Go ahead, Mr. Paris."

He pulled up on the hard plastic clasp and a snap echoed faintly through the sickbay. Ensign Berggren snorted in his sleep, coughed, and rolled over. Instantaneously a body appeared on the table and Paris could see the end of the belt he'd been holding.

The body belonged to a man as large as a Klingon warrior. He had orange hair and well-defined muscles. His chin was large, as Kjanders's was, and his forehead small. His face was cut with the same sand and wind burns as Paris's.

The man had a jury-rigged sling on one shoulder and he wore a black body suit. His eyes were set wide on his face and his nose was pointed. He wore eight-fingered black gloves. The wide black plastic belt looked more like a control panel with pockets than it did anything else. Faint orange lights blinked on the belt, and at first glance Paris could tell it did far more than just shield the guy.

"He is a professional at the task he was doing," Tuvok said after a moment of studying the ghost.

"It seems that way," Janeway said. She stood back and indicated that Doc Zimmerman should come forward. "What's wrong with him?"

"Besides his intense desire to not be seen," Doc Zimmerman said, "I don't have a clue. But give me a little room and I might be able to tell you."

Both Paris and Tuvok stepped back and Doc Zimmerman scanned the alien. "He has a badly sprained shoulder, a concussion, three broken ribs, and a crushed shoulder blade. The suit that he's wearing apparently stopped him from bleeding to death. He will live."

"How long until we can talk to him?" Janeway asked.

"One hour." Doc Zimmerman pointed to that belt. "And please take that off of him. It seems far too dangerous to be in this room."

Paris lifted the man's midsection while Tuvok slid the belt out and draped it over his arm.

"Now go away," Doc Zimmerman said. "I will call

you as soon as he wakes up." Then he looked at Tuvok and Paris. "And you two will not be allowed back in here in that condition."

"Are you ordering me to take a shower?" Paris asked. He had never been so thrilled to hear an order in his life.

"I have never in my career or in the careers of all the other doctors whose lives I have incorporated seen anyone so very filthy," Doc Zimmerman said.

"He's ordering us to take a shower," Paris said to Tuvok. "Can you believe it?"

"Make that captain's orders, also," Janeway said, and smiled.

"Thank you, Captain," Tuvok said.

Paris glanced at him, then did a double take. The Vulcan actually looked relieved.

# CHAPTER
# 21

Drickel slowly opened his eyes, trying to focus on the light overhead. His head throbbed and the light in his eyes added little needles into that pain.

"Awake? Good." The voice was male and crisp. The word "good" almost sounded like a command.

A blurry face appeared over Drickel and he fought to focus on it without success. The face moved away and Drickel tried to follow it, but the pain made him moan and close his eyes.

"Captain," the voice said. "Your formerly invisible man is now awake. His pain should be clearing enough in the next few minutes for you to talk to him."

"Thank you, Doctor. I'm on my way."

Drickel noticed that the man Captain had called Doctor was right about the pain. It was fading. He moved his head back and forth. The throbbing was subsiding into a dull ache, a little less pain than just a few moments before.

"If you remain still for two more minutes, I think you'll find life much more pleasant."

"All right." Drickel croaked the words. His mouth was dry and full of grit. He closed his eyes and lay still as the voice had commanded him.

He seemed to be on the Planet-Hoppers' ship. That idea somewhat frightened him. He couldn't imagine being that far above the planet's surface, let alone being out in space. From everything he'd heard about space it was a very dangerous place. The Planet-Hoppers were insane beings even to travel there.

At least they had a medical facility. The failure of the antigravity devices and the injury from the old wreck almost falling on him must have jarred loose his belt, or broken his invisibility shield so that they found him. It was obviously lucky for him that they had. Even if his injuries hadn't been serious, he wouldn't have been able to survive in that cold and wind. Severe-weather gear only protected for so long.

Something hissed—and the hiss sounded manufactured. It was followed by three sets of footsteps. He opened his eyes. The light still shone in them, but it didn't hurt this time. The pain had receded. He could even focus on the ceiling.

"How is he?" the woman's voice asked.

"He will live," the doctor said.

Drickel pushed himself up on one elbow. He was still wearing his body suit but his belt was gone. His suit was also cleaner than it had been since he reached this time.

The medical facility had an antiseptic look. It was done in dull blues and grays, apparently for Planet-Hopper comfort. Displays and monitors on the walls flashed at him. A man slept in another bunk, his snores a faint but present sound.

Drickel looked up at the four Planet-Hoppers. Pointed Ears and his pale companion were staring down at him. Up close their features looked delicate. Pointed Ears had an intent look and his pale companion a slight grin. They had not a speck of dirt on them and gave off the faint scent of soap.

A man with no hair stood beside them. He held a small scanner and was monitoring Drickel. For a moment Drickel's gaze remained on the man—no hair! Amazing. Such a thing never happened on Alcawell. Not in all the Periods put together—then Drickel realized he was staring. Finally he turned his attention to the fourth person.

She was apparently the captain he had heard a few moments before. She was slender and shorter than the men who surrounded her, but her clear blue eyes had intelligence and her expression wore its authority well. Her hair was a very tame brown, but the color suited her. Even the red on her uniform seemed more vibrant than the other colors he had seen in this place.

"How are you feeling?" she asked.

"I'm alive. I assume that's thanks to your people."

The captain nodded toward Pointed Ears and his pale companion. "Lieutenants Tuvok and Paris found you." She pointed to the other man. "This is our doctor, and I'm Captain Janeway. You are on the Federation *Starship Voyager.*"

Starship? They called these things starships. The word evoked night skies filled with stars, warm jungle air around him, and birds chirping in nearby trees. Some poetry, then, to these people.

"Nice to meet you, Captain," Drickel said. Then he looked directly at the two men. "Thank you for saving my life."

Paris said, "You're welcome."

Tuvok bowed slightly.

"We have questions we need to ask," the captain said, moving closer to him. Her voice was sharp, firm, and commanding. She stood with her hands clasped behind her back, her posture erect but not rigid. Her movements also implied a great physical strength.

"Ask away," Drickel said. If this was anything like Control, the more he said the better off he would be. He didn't know if Planet-Hoppers had rules the way Alcawell did, but he suspected they might. "Mind if I sit up first?"

Janeway glanced at the doctor.

"Why are my patients always eager to damage themselves?" he muttered.

"Doctor?" Janeway said.

"I'm sure it will be fine. I'm sure you should all diagnose yourselves." He glared at Paris and Tuvok. "At least you two are finally clean."

Drickel suppressed a smile and swung his feet off the table so he could face the Planet-Hoppers more directly. He patted the waist of his jumpsuit. It felt odd without the weight of the belt. "Does anyone know where my belt ended up?"

Tuvok nodded. "We had to remove it so that you

would become visible. Since the belt obviously had other components, some of which might be dangerous, we placed it in a containment field in Cargo Bay One."

"It was still working when you found me?" Drickel was actually shocked. If the invisibility device was still working, then there was no way they could have seen through the shield. These people were even more amazing than he had imagined. "How did you—?"

"There will be time enough for that later," the captain said. "But first I'd like some information about my away team. I need to know where they are being held and how we get them back to *Voyager*."

Drickel heard her words, but didn't understand them. "'Away team'?"

"Three of my crew were accidentally taken by that shuttle down there just after we first arrived here," she said. "It returned seconds later with a Mr. Kjanders on board. He said that my crew was being held by Control in the past and may be executed. I assume you are working for that Control since you were trying to scare us off."

Drickel tilted his head back. So that was the Time Alarm that Red had mentioned. He hadn't put those two elements together. All that work Drickel had done to protect the live shuttle had been wasted. He had arrived too late. The Planet-Hoppers had already triggered the shuttle. This entire mission from start to end had been a disaster.

The captain was watching him closely. Behind her scrutiny he could see concern for her crew. It was that concern that convinced him he'd better lay this all out. "I know nothing about your away team," he said. "And that's the truth."

"Then why were you trying to scare us away?" Paris asked.

"Because that is my job as defined by the Watchman Regulation Acts numbers 00000 to 49,000, all sections and subsections. We make certain that no Period is violated by a Planet-Hopper, or anyone else for that matter."

"I hate that term," Paris muttered.

"I do work for Control," Drickel continued, ignoring him, "but in a very special force we call the Back Room. Our job, simply, is to guard these old abandoned time-shuttle stations from intruders. I do this in fifty Periods."

"So your race did not just abandon this Period," Tuvok said. "Your people died out at some point?"

Drickel laughed. "Oh, no. Actually, we moved—"

"Gentlemen," the captain said. "This is all well and good, but it can wait until we've recovered the away team."

"Your away team as you call them is in serious trouble," Drickel said. "If you will allow me to explain a few things."

He rubbed a hand over his face.

"It appears that my patient is growing tired," the doctor said. "If you would all leave him—"

"No," Drickel said. "I'm fine. I'm just trying to figure out how to compress thousands of years and even more regulations into a few sentences." He frowned at Tuvok. "You people are quite sophisticated. I assume you have time travel?"

"Our people have done it, but it is very rudimentary. We prefer travel in space. No one in our culture regularly travels through time," he said.

"I think what Tuvok is saying," Paris said, "is that the more you explain the better off we'll be."

"As long as it goes to helping my away team," the captain said.

"And doesn't exhaust you too much," the doctor said. "No matter how strong your body is, it came close to failing you today. You must remember that."

Drickel wouldn't forget that. It was probably time to approach Control about Watchmen teams. He sighed. That meant even more regulation.

"Let me explain why you found an empty planet," Drickel said. "You already understand paradoxes, but there is a level beyond paradoxes in time travel. A level that we didn't discover for many years."

He scooted back on the table and crossed his legs. His hip seemed to be better too. The doctor frowned at him. The look was almost menacing. That bare scalp made him appear sinister.

"About one hundred and fifty thousand years ago Real Time from here," Drickel said, "we discovered that, for each decision point in Real Time, two or more alternate universes branch off depending on the number of solutions. Most of the time these branches simply blend back together like water running around a rock. But other times the branches form two or more distinct time lines. We discovered how to easily cross the boundaries between those time lines and in so doing discovered millions and millions of uninhabited time lines where our race never developed on this planet."

"So your race moved." Tuvok said. "Fascinating."

Drickel smiled at Tuvok. He liked old Pointed Ears. The man was quick. "At this very point in Real Time there are estimated to be over two hundred billion members of my race occupying over eight million alternate time lines."

"I fail to understand how this affects my away team," the captain said.

"It affects them in this way," Drickel said. "When Control discovered the dimensional shifts, the need to regulate our society became fierce. We already had strict regulations about time travel, but those regulations now had to protect the dimensions as well. Travel into the future became even more dangerous, and Control became even more rigid."

"Shifted to another dimension, are you?" the captain said.

"No," Drickel said. "Those shuttles below were designed before we knew about parallel universes. The ships return to the corresponding Real Time in the past. It was a logical protection once. But the regulations have changed. Your away team got on one of our shuttles, went to the past, and broke the law through no fault of their own."

"It is logical that a society like yours would establish unbreakable time guidelines," Tuvok said.

"But we are not part of that society," Janeway said.

"True," Drickel said. "But your crew could have discussed the future Alcawell with people in the past.

Each slip in the stream is extremely dangerous. That is why I work so hard at keeping Planet-Hoppers away from the ships."

"Good for you," Janeway said, "but I need to know if you can free them."

These people were quite intelligent. The rumors he had heard about Planet-Hoppers were clearly skewed. He felt a bit embarrassed by his explanation, as if he had been insulting their intelligence without meaning to.

"We might be able to free them," he said. "I'd need to get back to my time shuttle and report in."

"The one in the underground cavern?" Tuvok asked.

"You found that, also?" He glanced around. "You are the only Planet-Hoppers who ever beat me. And then you saved my life." He shook his head. "I am not only impressed, but I am also grateful. It seems only logical that I try to save your crew members."

Drickel moved his shoulders and arms a little, amazed that even his shoulder felt almost as good as new. "Doctor, when can I leave?"

"You need at least two more days of rest before you will be in good shape. Your body needs time to recover from the shock. Your physique is different enough from the others in my files that if you did have an infection, I might not be able to find it. To be safe, I would order bed rest for a week." The doctor sighed and glanced at Janeway. "But I understand that you—and all of my patients except the hapless Ensign Berggren, who seems content to snore his life away in sickbay—have busy lives to lead, and can't afford to take care of yourselves. That being the case—" The doctor wiped his hands together as if shaking Drickel off them."—the sooner you leave, the better."

"Will do, Doc," Paris said.

"We can beam you directly to your shuttle," Janeway said. She faced Drickel. "If you don't mind, we'll accompany you."

Drickel laughed and stepped down off the medical table. "I would expect nothing else." He hesitated. "Oh, and Captain? You mentioned a person named Kjanders?"

The captain nodded. "He showed up on the shuttle that took our crew and seemed genuinely shocked at what he found."

Drickel laughed. "I suppose he was. If it's the same Kjanders I've heard of, he is a known criminal sought by Control. I would be careful."

The captain smiled, the first real smile from her Drickel had seen. It softened her face. "We guessed as much. At the moment, he is imbibing too much coffee in our officers' mess. We've kept him under constant surveillance."

Drickel shook his head in amazement again. It would be good to have these Planet-Hoppers as friends. He sure wouldn't want to be against them again.

"Would someone please turn off my program?" the doctor said.

"Emergency medical program off," Tuvok said.

The doctor faded away.

Drickel pointed at where the doctor had been. He was shocked. Totally shocked. "I was cured by a—"

"Hologram," the captain said.

"An invisible man healed by a holographic doctor," Paris said. "That seems logical to me. How about you, Tuvok?"

"I see nothing strange about it," Tuvok said. "We have a holographic doctor and Mr. Drickel was invisible. These things happen."

Paris laughed, followed by the captain. Drickel wasn't sure what the two of them found so funny. Apparently Tuvok didn't know either. These Planet-Hoppers were very talented but very strange people.

# CHAPTER

# 22

JANEWAY DID NOT MOVE AS THE TRANSPORTER BEAMS RE-
leased her. Paris and Tuvok had warned her about the
dust in the caverns. They had arrived before her and
Drickel, and were already holding up lanterns to
illuminate the underground room.

The dust was thick and the air was very dry. It
sucked the moisture from her mouth and nose immediately. Paris had said that the caverns were warmer
than the surface, but they still weren't warm. They
were at freezing, if she had to lay a wager on it.

Everything in the room was covered with dust. The
beams of lights cut circles through the darkness, but
the blackness still lurked at the edges. What looked to
be the remains of a workstation was buried under
dust. The only thing that looked new was a device
near one side of the room.

Tuvok and Paris had trained their lights in that direction.

The device was human-sized. It had a bench seat and a control panel and was the only thing not deep in dust.

"Do not move very fast." Tuvok reminded them. "This dust is very light and can be stirred up easily."

"I'll just stand here and be a lamppost," Paris said, holding the lamp up high.

Drickel and Janeway glanced at each other, then walked side by side to the time shuttle. The dust floated like tiny moths around them. Paris coughed.

"Dammit, Tuvok," he said. "The doctor is going to order us to take showers again."

Janeway smiled.

Drickel moved over to the time shuttle. Without sitting down, he touched a few buttons. The dust caught up to him and Janeway, swirling around them like a friendly whirlwind. Some of it caught in her mouth. The dust had an alkaline taste. She was glad that Tuvok had already tested it.

Drickel hunched so that the swirling dust stayed away from his mouth. "Emergency override. Intra-period Communication. Drickel to Noughi, citing Watchman Regulations 500 through 537, all Sections. Noughi, are you there?"

"Watchman Back Room Response via Emergency Override rules at Control, Items 999 through 1500. Noughi here. This better be good, Drickel. You just caused me a month of regulation citing." A woman's voice came through after only a moment's pause.

The hair rose on the back of Janeway's neck. That

woman was speaking from the past as easily as Janeway spoke to *Voyager*. She was hearing a voice three hundred thousand years old.

"Probably more than a month," Drickel said. His voice actually some lightness to it. Was he flirting? "Whoever popped my alarm sent me here late. The Planet-Hoppers I was supposed to chase away had already lost three of their crew to your section several Real Time hours before I appeared."

"Sounds like you're the one who gets to file the complaint, Drickel." The woman chuckled. "We'll have forms 7564.555 through 32,889.321 sent to your home system so that you can work on this problem when you return." Then she paused. "If this is what you caused an Emergency Override for, I will make sure you get extra forms to process."

"No," Drickel said. "There's some problems here. What happened to those three crew members?"

"They came through here. They were Rawlik's first. He spent too much Real Time on this case. He got a slap from Control. Overriders Regulations S-Series, Numbers 2A through 37B, Personal Involvement Sections 1 and 2, you know."

"I know," Drickel said. "I've been slapped with that before."

Janeway had lost the thread of the numbers long ago. All she knew was that Drickel sounded a bit disappointed.

"You should've been here, though, Drickel. I can understand why he lost track of the regulations, you know. Those Planet-Hoppers caused more Time Alarms than any prisoners previously."

"Did they cause one when I went through Eight-eighty-nine?"

"Yes, and three more after that."

Drickel turned his head a little and grinned at Janeway. "With that much activity, then, they're still alive, right?"

Silence greeted him. Janeway held her breath.

"Sorry, Drickel. You missed the execution by three Real Time hours. Red tells me they're still not back to work out there in the main room."

Janeway felt as if someone had punched her solidly in the stomach. Beside her Paris sucked in a sharp breath.

Torres. Kim. Neelix. She couldn't believe they were dead. She just couldn't.

Paris groaned behind her, and his light wavered. Tuvok remained steady. Drickel held up one finger as if indicating that they should all wait.

"Are you certain, Noughi? Sometimes the orders get made, but the executions take a few Real Time days."

"Days?" She said. "Try weeks. It took a dozen different tries and an entire committee to outwit those people. Finally Rawlik had to back-time to poison them."

"Oh, man," Drickel said. "And they're still thinking of slapping him with a Personal Involvement?"

"I'm afraid so," the woman said. "Look, if we stay on this any longer we will have thirty more forms to complete."

"All right," Drickel said. "Keep those forms ready. I might have to get back to you."

"Wonderful," the woman said. With a flick of a light, her voice disappeared from the chamber.

Drickel braced one hand against the device and rested his forehead against his arm. Then he stood. "I'm sorry," he said. "I really am."

Janeway let out the breath she had been holding. She was hoping he would have more for her than that. She turned away from him and walked slowly over near the door. The light from the lanterns cast shadows down the dust-filled hallway. Three sets of footprints led off into the dark. She thought that somehow fitting for the moment.

She just couldn't accept that her crew members were dead. Not this way. Not now. This was all so stupid.

If she had pulled them off the shuttle sooner or sent a team into the past sooner, they might still be here. There were so many ifs she wanted to go back and change. So many things she wanted to do differently, if she only had the chance.

Time Alarm. Back-timing, as Kjanders called it. She was standing three hundred thousand years after her crew was killed. What difference was a short three hours?

She whirled so quickly the dust stormed and swirled up around her. She brushed it away from her face and moved into the open. "Explain to me what she meant by Time Alarm."

Drickel's expression became guarded for a moment.

"Ah, hell," Paris said. "We just lost three of our best people. You can answer the woman's questions."

Drickel shrugged. "A Time Alarm," he said, "is

when Control must send a force or a person back a very short distance in time to stop something from happening. It is rarely done, and causing a Time Alarm is a death-penalty offense. Your crew caused four of them besides the original eight-hundred violation. That's something amazing. You have very talented people working with you, Captain."

"Had," Paris said. His light was quivering.

"Tom," Janeway said softly. She made sure there was an element of command in that tone as well as compassion. "Mr. Drickel, tell me why Time Alarms are so rare."

"Beside the obvious dangers of creating a time paradox," Drickel said, glancing at Tuvok, "each back-timing causes another dimension to branch off from the point of changed action. Ideally the other dimension is so minutely different from the first that it makes no difference to society."

"And if it does make a difference?"

"Then another time stream is created," Drickel said, "along with more people who might ultimately spread out through the dimensions in the future."

Janeway nodded. The idea she had was getting more and more concrete. "But nothing worse than that will happen?"

Drickel looked puzzled. "Not unless a time paradox is set up. Or in worse cases, a permanent time loop where the people involved are doomed to repeat the event over and over. But back-timing is usually done over such short time frames that that rarely happens."

"All right," Janeway said. She moved slowly back across the dusty room. She was coated in the gray stuff. It felt sticky and uncomfortable. She stopped next to Drickel, put her hands on her hips, and looked up at him. "You said you wanted to help. Here's your chance." She pointed to his time shuttle. "Can you make that shift back exactly enough hours so that I can warn my crew not to enter that shuttle?"

Drickel went so pale as to earn his ghostly appellation. His features in the lantern light and floating dust almost appeared haunted. "That would create two universes. One where your crew died and you moved on, and one where they lived."

"Simply by asking that question, Captain, you have created other universes," Tuvok said. "In one universe Drickel will say no and one he will say yes."

Janeway nodded. Tuvok was right, of course. Her question had created the alternate universe. She had to try a slightly different tack. "Will the execution of my crew members make any long-term difference to your society?"

Drickel thought for a moment and then nodded. "The other universe will still exist and move forward without your crew members."

Janeway caught how he phrased that statement and glanced at Tuvok, who also had caught it. Drickel had said "the other universe," which meant he would help make it right in this one.

"So you'll help us?" Janeway asked.

Drickel smiled. "I'll try. But I'm not sure we will succeed."

"And thus," Tuvok said, "even more alternate dimensions are created."

"This is giving me a headache," Paris said. "Let's

just go get Kim and the others and go on with our lives, and not worry about our other lives which we, apparently, are not living?"

Janeway laughed and turned to Drickel. "Yes, let's."

"Captain," Tuvok said. "It will not work."

She turned to face her security officer. "Why not?" she demanded. She could tell that she had asked far too loudly, as her voice echoed in the long-dead room.

"It would set up a paradox," Tuvok said. "And possibly a time loop in which we would be stuck forever."

"Explain." She didn't want to hear the answer. She only wanted to hear what would save her away team, bring them back from the dead.

"For example," Tuvok said, his voice calm as always. "You and Mr. Drickel return to the point just before the away team boarded the shuttle. You stop them. At that point in time *two* of the both of you exist in that universe. You, Captain, in the ship and on the shuttle, and you, Mr. Drickel, at a time right before you were sent here as well as on that shuttle."

Drickel sighed. "Tuvok, you continue to astonish me. It took me eight months of time school before I managed that concept, and apparently I still forget about it."

He coughed and brushed dust off his face. "This, of course, creates an additional problem. After we warn your crew members, this universe does not exist. Where would we return to? If we warn them, then we never met, therefore we couldn't have warned them. I was taught that basic 'killing your grandfather' principle in field training. A time paradox is formed when the two time streams, or dimensions, flow apart and a person is trapped in the wrong one."

Tuvok nodded. "That is the logic of it, I am afraid."

Anger rose in Janeway's stomach and lodged in her throat. She longed for Torres. B'Elanna often expressed the anger they all felt. "So," Janeway said as calmly as she could, "if that isn't possible, how do we save the away team?"

"I am afraid," Tuvok said, "that if the action to save them has not already happened in this time line, it will never happen."

Drickel nodded.

"I refuse to accept that," Janeway said. "We have all of time at our disposal."

"But, Captain," Tuvok said. "We also have a society to think of."

She knew that. She knew that with the same bone-deep certainty she had had when she had stared in the face of the Prime Directive and decided to strand her people in the Delta Quadrant rather than take the easy route home. She would not, could not, hurt Alcawell, but she had to find a solution.

Had to.

"When we're looking at millions of years," Paris said, "we're only talking about messing with a fraction of a fraction of time. Surely—"

"Such a simple suggestion," Drickel said, not letting him finish, "is a felony in my culture."

"Logical," Tuvok said.

Janeway walked back to the door leading down the long dark hallway. She didn't care how much dust she kicked up. Her future would always have that dark hallway ahead of it. She had lost other crew members in the past and she would lose more in the future. It was the curse of command. And each loss would have a long dark hallway leading from it into her nightmares.

Dust floated peacefully in the air around her. She leaned her head against the cold stone of the wall and just tried to breathe.

There had to be a way.

There had to be.

The silence stretched to a minute before finally Drickel broke it. "Captain," he said, his voice echoing in the small chamber.

She turned around to see Drickel leaning against his machine and both Tuvok and Paris standing holding lanterns. The dust in the air gave the small room almost a surreal feeling.

"There might be a way without creating a paradox."

"How?" she demanded, moving back closer to him and sending more waves of dust into the air as she did.

"Tuvok is correct. If the action hasn't already been taken in this time line, it won't be. And the only way to discover that is to ask Control to do the back-timing."

"Control is the authority who killed my away team. Now you want to ask them?"

"Actually," Drickel said, "only one member of Control. Rawlik."

She glanced at Tuvok and he shrugged, indicating that he had no idea what Drickel's idea was. So she turned to Drickel and took a deep breath. "Explain."

Drickel nodded. "My suggestion is that we trust the

system. It seems that notwithstanding our surroundings, the system, and therefore Control, works. And will continue to work for hundreds of thousands of years."

Tuvok nodded. "Logical."

"I'm beginning to hate that phrase," Paris said.

"Rawlik is a friend of mine. He's the one who convinced me to join the Back Room when I got into some trouble early in my life. I know for a fact that this is the first execution he's had to perform and it will be tearing him up inside. In fact, he was already cited for spending too much time on this, trying to save your crew. He would be grateful for a chance to do just that."

"He should have just opened the door, then," Paris said.

"Tom." This time Janeway's voice held a warning. "I'm sorry, Mr. Drickel. We all have close friends on that team. Please continue."

"Noughi said they were poisoned. I might be able to convince Rawlik to reduce the amount of poison and—"

"And I claim the bodies," Janeway said, excitement coming back into her soul. "In this way, it would appear to all concerned that the team died, but no one actually would."

"And this would not set up a time paradox," Tuvok said.

"But convincing Rawlik will be another matter," Drickel said. "I would do it in a heartbeat. At most, he could get another Personal Involvement citation. Most people at his level of command collect a dozen of them before enforcement becomes routine. But I cannot speak for him. And there is another problem."

Janeway nodded. "If I go back, I risk my life as well."

Her words floated in the room like the dust. She looked at Tuvok. He said nothing, which was as close to actual approval as she would get.

Paris leaned toward her. "I'll go, Captain. I don't mind the risk."

"Neither do I, Mr. Paris." She smiled at him. "And I have had more training in diplomacy than you." She tapped her comm badge. "Commander Chakotay?"

"Yes, Captain." His comforting voice filled the room. She hadn't realized until just that moment how comforting his voice was to her and how much she depended on him.

"I will be accompanying Mr. Drickel into the past. Tuvok and Paris will explain."

"Are you convinced this is the only way, Captain? I would be glad to—"

"This is the only way, Commander," she said, her voice firm yet gentle. "Thank you. If I do not return, your orders are to leave orbit and continue for home. You are not to send another rescue team. If this doesn't work, nothing will. Understood?"

"How long should we wait, Captain?"

She turned to Drickel.

"We'll be back in ten minutes in this time frame if we're coming back," Drickel said. "We may spend months getting through all the regulations and paperwork, but in this time we will return in ten minutes. That's as close as Noughi would dare time it."

"If you do take months, you'll never remember it," Tuvok said.

Janeway gave Tuvok a puzzled look. That logic made no sense to her, so she continued. "Chakotay, leave orbit in two hours, taking as many raw materials as you can load on board from the old shuttles."

"Understood, Captain." There was a slight pause. "And good luck."

"Thanks."

She turned to Drickel. "Let's do it."

"We'll be waiting right here, Captain," Paris said, "to help when you get back."

"Thank you, Mr. Paris." She looked over her shoulder at Tuvok. He nodded, which was all she needed.

Drickel was waiting, hovering above his seat. He indicated a place beside him and she climbed in. There were no real controls in front of her. Nothing but what looked to be a simple keyboard.

Drickel reached over and punched a button. "Standard communication, Codes 15 to 36. Hi, Noughi. Two coming home to you."

"Ready and waiting," Noughi said. "Oh, boy. More paperwork."

He sat down.

Janeway braced herself as the lantern-lit dusty room vanished.

# CHAPTER
# 23

JANEWAY BLINKED AS HER EYES ADJUSTED TO THE BRIGHT light. She coughed dust from her lungs, glad she didn't have to work in the darkness of the caverns forever.

The room that the shuttle had brought her and Drickel to seemed smaller than the one Janeway had just left. It had an odd sweet smell. A single desk sat to one side, covered with a drooping fern. A large workstation filled with computers, flashing lights, and a scrolling list of regulations was the wall to Janeway's right.

Drickel held her arm so that she remained in the booth until the shuttle settled. A heavyset middle-aged man wearing a bright—almost neon red—wig grinned at Drickel.

"Man, you sure like doing reports," he said.

Drickel grinned in return.

A woman approached the booth. "Well," she said. "I don't."

Janeway recognized her voice. Noughi. She was as slight as the man was large, and on her the extended chin and tiny forehead of these people looked startlingly attractive. She wore a black shirt layered over a white one. They were opened at the collars and cuffs, but shiny buttons indicated that the fashion could go either way. Her tight leggings tied at the ankles and on her tiny feet she wore the largest, most useless pair of shoes that Janeway had ever seen.

"Captain Janeway," Drickel said. "This is Noughi, and my good friend Red."

Red was certainly well named. Janeway nodded to both of them. Then she looked at Drickel. He was flirting with Noughi. Another side to him. A side Janeway liked.

"Welcome," Noughi said. She didn't even totter on those amazing shoes. "Your people were fabulous. Outside the Back Room, minor 'crats were laying wagers on how many Time Alarms would sound before Control managed to outfox them."

Janeway suppressed a shudder. These people had built up so many rules and regulations that they often forgot they were dealing with living beings.

"Noughi," Red said, with a bit of reprimand in his voice. "This woman has come to recover them."

Noughi blushed. The color that rose in her skin was a dull yellow, which clashed with the white of her underblouse. "I didn't mean to insult—"

"You didn't," Janeway said. "It's nice to know some people here were pulling for my team."

"You headed for Period One, I assume?" Red said to Drickel.

Drickel nodded. "Would you tell Rawlik we're coming?"

"Be glad to," Noughi said. "Good luck."

"I'll walk you to the shuttle," Red said.

They left through a door Janeway hadn't even seen on the side of the room. She almost wished she had brought Tuvok here. He would have been fascinated by the look of these caverns three hundred thousand years in the past.

The hallways were still stone, but there was no dust. She patted herself, and dust came off her. She must look a fright. No matter. Soon she would have her crew and be able to return to *Voyager.*

The corridor they entered had the faint scent of burning pitch. They had entered at a fork. She looked over her shoulder down the other fork. Trees lined the walls and were probably the source of the scent.

They they stepped into a side room that seemed oddly familiar to Janeway. The room was wide and tall and the stone had a flat, utilitarian feel, although the floor was covered with concrete that had long since been covered by dust.

One ship sat in the center of that floor. The ship was a miniature version of the shuttles that were on the surface. It lacked the long landing legs, and the tall ramp, and its circumference was smaller, but its design was essentially the same.

Drickel opened the ramp. Red moved close to him. "You're taking quite a risk that Rawlik will work with you, friend," he said.

Drickel grinned. "I specialize in risk, Red. You know that."

"Well," Red said, "for what it's worth, I'm cheering for you."

Drickel grasped Red's hand in a formal gesture. "It's worth a lot."

Then he climbed inside. Janeway followed.

The small craft had ten seats and no apparent controls. There was no one else on board.

Drickel took a deep breath and smiled at Janeway. Then he sat down. Janeway did as well.

The seat was softer than she had expected, yet it didn't invite comfort. A moment after she sat, the door thumped closed. The ship lifted off the platform and gently returned to the same place.

"Was there a problem?" Janeway asked.

"No," Drickel said. "You've just traveled over four hundred million years into the past."

Janeway still had the dust from the future on her clothing. These time distances seemed so fantastic to her that she had no real conception of them. Yet she did feel very far away from Paris, Tuvok, and *Voyager*.

It took the door longer to open than it had taken them to travel in time. When it did, Drickel stood and walked to the ramp. Janeway did the same.

If she hadn't known she had traveled in time, she wouldn't have been able to tell at first glance. The room appeared the same—the single shuttle, the concrete floor, the stone corridor leading away. Only the cast outside the ship had changed.

Several people wearing orange suits stood near the corridor door. Before them a man who had the same general build as Paris stood waiting, his hands behind his back. He had the characteristic Alcawellian features, but on his large chin, he wore a goatee. His hair was brown and he had apparently forgone the wig that was custom to his people.

Beside him were three long black boxes.

Apparently coffins looked the same on every world.

Janeway put a hand to her forehead, feeling momentarily dizzy. Drickel had said she might spend three months here, fighting their bureaucracy. Well, she'd stay years if she had to.

Drickel hesitated at the sight of the coffins. Then his hesitation changed. A smile played at his lips. "Success," he whispered to Janeway. "Let me do most of the talking."

Drickel came forward, his hand out, and he and Rawlik repeated the gesture that he and Red had just done. "Thanks for meeting us," Drickel said.

"You know," Rawlik said, "you're causing me two extra Personal Involvement citations."

"You might want to go to the Regulation Bureau," Drickel said. "The rules on dispensing bodies to the families should be the same for Planet-Hoppers as they are for Alcawellians."

Rawlik shook his head. "I've had enough red tape for this Real Time year." A smile hovered around his mouth as well.

Janeway's throat was dry. Drickel had said they had success, but she didn't know how he could tell. Her uniform was still covered with dust from the future, and those coffins looked very, very real.

Janeway walked to Drickel's side.

"Captain," Rawlik said, and Janeway almost jumped. She hadn't been introduced. This man acted as if he knew her. Perhaps he did.

He took her hand in his warm one. "Let me express my sympathies for the fate of your crew." His voice was louder than it needed to be. "Our laws are harsh, but they are just. We protect our society as best we can."

No answer was probably the best answer. It was good that she hadn't allowed Paris to come in her place. He probably would have expressed to Rawlik and his companions his exact opinion of bureaucracy. And Paris didn't handle *flexible* bureaucracies well. He wouldn't have tolerated this one at all.

Rawlik was still holding her hand, and something had dug into her palm. He was giving her something. It took all of her control not to look at her hand in surprise.

Then he let go. She cupped her palm. He had given her a piece of paper.

Rawlik turned to the people in orange. "Load the coffins," he said. "The captain is here to claim her dead."

The orange suits picked up the coffins and carried them like garish pallbearers into the shuttle. A shudder ran down Janeway's back. She had hoped she would never witness this, but always knew she would.

A captain lost crew.

That was part of the risk.

After they had placed the coffins inside, the orange

suits left the shuttlebay. Rawlik took a step closer to her and spoke softly. "Captain, you have the antidote in your hand. We had to use a drug that simulated death. Couldn't reduce the dosage because it would have been too obvious. I'm afraid you only have an hour Real Time, otherwise they will truly die."

"Will that be enough?" Janeway asked Drickel.

He nodded. "If we move now."

"I can't thank you enough," Janeway said to Rawlik.

He grinned. "Actually, it was my pleasure. Working with Drickel and you these last few months felt like the old days, and we got to do some good."

Drickel chuckled. "I told you not to take that desk job," he said.

Rawlik shrugged. "It has its benefits."

"This is one," Drickel said to Rawlik. "Tell me, how long did it take us to get this through the council?"

"Three months Real Time."

"Three months?" Janeway said. "I've been here three months?"

"Yes," Rawlik said. "And we even found time to help you clean that dust off your uniform."

She smiled too.

"Go now," he said. "You're losing Real Time."

Janeway nodded. "Thank you. And thank Control."

"You already did," he said and smiled. "Very eloquently, I might add."

Drickel took her arm, and together they went up the ramp. The coffins sat just inside the door, grim and dark.

"Oh, one more thing," Rawlik said. He came close

to the ramp, Janeway crouched so that she could hear him. "Please tell Torres that I was only doing my job."

Janeway nodded and squeezed his hand. "As are we all."

She entered the shuttle, trailing her fingers on the polished surface of all three coffins. The paper was safely tucked in her left hand. "Let's go, Mr. Drickel."

"Sit down," he said. "This thing won't go otherwise."

She sat beside him and stared at the coffins. She could almost hear the hour ticking away around her.

The door closed, the shuttle rose and then landed softly. Such an easy way to travel. And so very quick. The door opened, and Red was where they had left him.

Only more orange suits stood around him. His hair clashed with their outfits.

"Let's move," Drickel said. "We only have permission to allow this Planet-Hopper here for a few more Real Time minutes. These coffins go with her."

The orange suits grabbed the coffins like cordwood and hurried them to the door to the Back Room. Then they set them down.

"Security Regulation 111.42," Drickel said, as if that were explanation enough. At Janeway's confusion, he added, "They can't come in here."

In fact, Red waited until the orange suits were out of the corridor before opening the door. Noughi stood inside, her shoes on the desk. They looked like oddly shaped vases from that perspective. She came out and together the four of them carried the coffins inside the Back Room.

They loaded the first coffin onto the shuttle with Drickel aboard. The coffin barely fit within the confines of it, sliding across the seat beside Drickel.

"Get me at ten minutes from last departure," Drickel said. "I'll unload and come right back for the others."

"I'd like to go with you," Janeway said.

"Sorry," Noughi said. "This machine can only carry two large items at a time."

"Very well," Janeway said. Drickel had to go since she didn't know how to operate the machine. "Give this to Tuvok." She handed Drickel the paper with the antidote on it.

"Will do. I'll take care of things."

She nodded and stood back from the shuttle.

"What's the hurry?" Red asked. Then he glanced at the captain. "Man, I can be as callous as Noughi. And here I scolded her for that remark earlier."

Janeway smiled at him, making certain the smile had a sadness to it. "We just want to get our crew taken care of and get on with our mission."

Red nodded as Drickel gave Noughi the go ahead. He and the coffin disappeared. Thirty seconds Real Time later, which seemed like an eternity to Janeway, Drickel's voice said, "Noughi, pull me back."

A moment later he and the shuttle appeared.

He repeated the process twice more and then smiled at Janeway as he appeared again. He patted the seat beside him and said. "You ready to go back to your ship?"

"Absolutely," she said.

With a wave at Noughi and a quick shake of Red's hand, she climbed in beside Drickel.

Noughi looked at Drickel. "You're going to have to help me with all this paperwork," she said.

He smiled. "Gladly."

A moment later the very dusty room surrounded her. Paris was holding a lantern, looking like the lamppost he had said he would be. Except that he was coughing in the waves of dust.

He was the best thing she had seen in ages.

Literally.

# CHAPTER
# 24

JANEWAY HAD HERSELF, PARIS, AND DRICKEL BEAMED directly to sickbay. She couldn't wait to see if her team made it. As she materialized near the door she saw the doctor look up. He was standing near Kim, who was blinking groggily. Torres was sitting up. Neelix had one of Kes's hands trapped beneath his own and was talking softly to her.

Janeway smiled. They had made it.

They had survived.

"No, no, no," Doc Zimmerman said. "Absolutely not. Get out of here now. I warned you before, especially you, Mr. Paris. You would not be allowed in here again in that condition."

"I'll do double duty to clean this place," Paris said as he walked over to Kim. He clasped Kim's hand in a modified high-five. "Kid, you gotta stop going places without me. I'da got you outta that mess in an instant."

"Yeah, right," Torres said. "Mr. High and Mighty. You didn't face the Bureaucracy from Hell."

"You've never been in a Federation Penal Settlement," Paris said.

"I'm sorry, Doctor," Janeway said. "Let us see the away team and then we shall leave you alone."

Doc Zimmerman shook his head. "No understanding of medicine, no understanding of protocol, and no understanding of cleanliness. It's a wonder this place isn't a breeding ground for all sorts of exotic diseases." He picked up his tricorder and leaned over Kim again.

"My darling, you should have seen us," Neelix was saying to Kes in as soft a tone as he could manage. "We were brilliant. Never, they said, never had they known such daring, such persistence."

"I missed you, Neelix," Kes said. "I'm just glad you're back."

"Frankly, my darling, so am I. I thought of you constantly—"

"And spoke of you even more," Kim said.

"You will not move or speak until I tell you to," Doc Zimmerman snapped. "Now I have to run these readings all over again."

"Sorry, Doc," Kim said.

"I warned you—"

Janeway's smile grew. She had missed these people. She was very relieved to have them back. She tapped Drickel on the arm and nodded her thanks. He smiled as well. Then she went to Torres's side.

"How are you feeling?" Janeway asked.

Torres gave Drickel a questioning glance and then looked at the captain. "Very lucky to be alive, actually, Captain. how did you ever manage to beat that system? We tried everything."

Janeway glanced at Drickel. "It's a long story that I don't even know parts of. Suffice it to say that Mr. Drickel here backed you out."

"Back-timed." The word exploded from Torres. "I hope I never hear that word again." Then she looked up at Drickel. Her expression softened. "Thank you."

He bowed slightly. "You are more than welcome."

Janeway squeezed Torres's hand. "It's good to have you back."

"It's great to be back, Captain."

Janeway smiled at Torres.

Torres recognized her own about-face. "Believe me, Captain, after this experience, Starfleet looks almost good to me."

"Careful, Maquis," Kim said from the next bed, "you'll impeach yourself."

Torres laughed. "I'm sure the feeling will pass."

Janeway patted Torres's hand, leaving a small dusty smudge on her skin. "I need to clean up and then I will return," Janeway said. "It is wonderful to see you all looking well."

"Captain," Neelix said, "I think we can safely add this admonition to any away teams. No naps. Not ever."

Torres and Kim both laughed and Doc Zimmerman scowled.

"That sounds sensible, Mr. Neelix." Janeway

walked back to Drickel. He was watching the entire scene with a smile on his face.

"I assume you'll want to be going back soon," Janeway said, "but may I offer you one of our guest quarters so that you can clean up, and then give you a tour of the ship and a hot meal?"

"I'd love that, Captain," Drickel said. "But I'm not quite done with my business yet. There is the matter of Kjanders we might want to settle."

Kjanders. He had left her mind entirely. Janeway frowned. Another dilemma, and one she had best meet head-on. "Mr. Drickel, I have personal qualms about returning him to you knowing that he faces certain death."

"It's not quite so certain, Captain," Drickel said. "Actually, it's his choice."

"Choice?" Torres said from across the room. "How come we didn't get a choice?"

"If you are going to agitate my patients, you are going to have to leave," Doc Zimmerman said. "I can only tolerate this circus atmosphere for so long."

"Don't worry, Doc," Paris said. "If it gets too much for you, we'll just shut down your program."

"These people are out of danger, but they still need monitoring," Doc Zimmerman said. "Shutting down my program would be a bad idea at this time."

Kim and Paris burst into laughter. Doc Zimmerman looked confused.

Janeway didn't allow the interchange to distract her. "What type of choice are you going to give him?" she asked Drickel.

"I'm going to offer him a job."

"A job?" If Janeway had expected an answer it hadn't been that. "But you told me he was a wanted criminal."

"He is wanted for violations from five-hundred series to the eight-hundred series and probably some beyond. Very creative." Then Drickel grinned. "But not as creative as I was."

"You?" Janeway looked up at the alien face. She was honestly surprised.

He laughed. "Yes, me. In our society, the risk takers tend to get in trouble early because they fight the system. But it's those type of risk takers that can do my job very well."

"So you want to offer him a Watchman job like yours?"

Drickel nodded. "He'll have to survive the schooling, but I doubt he'll have much trouble with that if he's managed to elude Control as long as he has."

The captain looked at Torres, who was smiling. Janeway was glad she had the common decency to not laugh. "We are just learning the fact in our culture that sometimes the rebels make the best team members," Janeway said to Drickel. Then she looked at Torres again. "But we *are* learning it."

Torres nodded thank you and said nothing.

Janeway tapped her comm badge. "Mr. Kjanders, you are wanted in sickbay immediately."

"Um," Kjanders's voice responded, sounding confused. "Um, sure. I guess. Be right there."

He signed out.

Kes smiled at Janeway. "Kjanders has spent most of

his time in the officers' mess," she said. "He discovered that there was more than one kind of coffee."

"He didn't give you any trouble, did he?" Neelix sat up, obviously ready to do battle. With one hand, Doc Zimmerman pushed him back on the table.

"I only spoke to him once, Neelix," Kes said. "He was very polite."

The ship was back to normal. Janeway wiped a hand over her face. Layers of dust smudged around. She, Paris, and Drickel looked as if they had been mining sledge on Druvarious IV.

Then she remembered the message she still carried. "I almost forgot," she said. "B'Elanna, Mr. Rawlik said to tell you that he was only doing his job."

A faraway look came into Torres's eyes.

"I told him we all were," Janeway said.

Torres smiled. "Thank you, Captain."

Janeway noded.

At that moment Kjanders appeared in the door. He saw Drickel and his mouth opened wide.

"Control," he said. "How did Control get here?"

"That," Drickel said, "is something you will get to learn in the next few Real Time weeks. Can you excuse me, Captain?"

"Only if you take me up on that meal. And I would like to discuss the ruined shuttles below."

"We already discussed the shuttles," Drickel said.

"Briefly," Janeway said. "But I would like you to give some consideration to allowing us to take some interior plates from just a few of the old wrecks. We could use the resources in our journey home and considering the fate of the old wrecks, I don't think anything would be missed."

Drickel laughed. "In exchange for a good hot meal and good conversation, of course." He bowed to her again, then put an arm around Kjanders's shoulders as he led him to a corner of sickbay.

As they walked, Janeway heard Drickel recite several numbers. Kjanders stopped and said, "You want me to *what?!?*"

Then Janeway laughed. They just might have to stay in orbit another day Real Time before everything was resolved with Alcawell and the two Alcawellians. But she didn't mind. After all, on a journey of the length they faced, what was an extra day or so along the way?

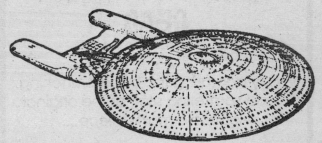